CATCH!

By
Jasmine Jones

HYPERION/**miramax books**
NEW YORK

Printed in the United States of America
First Edition
1 3 5 7 9 10 8 6 4 2

This book is set in 11.5/16.5 New Aster.
ISBN 0-7868-3769-1

Visit www.hyperionbooksforchildren.com

Visit BETTY & VERONICA® online at www.archiecomics.com

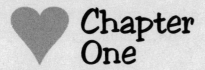# Chapter
One

"Hello, Daddykins!" Veronica Lodge said in a singsongy voice as she swept into the white marble entranceway of the family mansion.

"Veronica!" Mr. Lodge's eyes were round. "What on earth have you done?"

Veronica batted her long, glossy, black eyelashes innocently. "What do you mean?" she asked.

"I mean this!" Mr. Lodge roared as he pointed to the enormous heap of shopping bags at Veronica's feet.

Just then, the butler stumbled through the front door. He was struggling to keep his balance under the weight of the boxes piled in his arms.

"Just look!" Mr. Lodge cried. "You're going to send Smithers to the hospital, and me to the poorhouse."

"Oh, Daddykins, don't be silly," Veronica said,

effortlessly pulling the top few boxes from Smithers's pile and setting them neatly on a nearby table. "Mumsiekins and I just did a little shopping in Paris this weekend, that's all."

"Excuse me, Miss Lodge," Smithers said from behind his pile of boxes. "But should I take these up to your room?"

"Yes, please," Veronica replied. "We'll sort them out later."

Mr. Lodge shook his head and ran a hand through his mane of silver hair. "I never should have given you that credit card," he said with a groan.

"Of course you should have!" Veronica insisted. "I need it for emergencies."

Mr. Lodge rolled his eyes. "And I suppose you call these an emergency?" he asked, nodding to the stack of boxes.

Veronica stared at him. "Of course I do!" she cried. "Everything here was on sale!"

"Where is your mother?" Mr. Lodge demanded, just as an elegant woman with perfectly styled blond hair and dancing dark eyes walked into the front hall. Behind her were three men, each rolling a dolly holding a large trunk.

"Hello, darling!" chirped Mrs. Lodge to her husband. "Veronica and I had such a lovely trip to Paris!"

"Sweetheart, I—"

"Oh, you should have been there, darling," Mrs. Lodge went on. "Paris is so beautiful in the springtime."

"I wouldn't know," Mr. Lodge grumbled. "I was on a business trip, making money."

"Well, of course you were, Daddykins!" Veronica pouted, and her voice was edged with impatience. "Why do you think we went to Paris?"

Really, sometimes my father can be so impossible!

Her father raised an eyebrow. "Because you thought I might be there?"

"No, no. Because Mummy was so lonely here without you."

"That's right, dear," Mrs. Lodge agreed. "Ronnie and I missed you terribly."

"On Friday, she simply couldn't stand being in this big house without you. So I said, 'Mummy, why don't we go to Paris?'" Veronica grinned. "'The spring fashions should be in stores by now. You don't need to sit around this dreary house, thinking of Daddykins.'"

Mr. Lodge's eyebrows knit together in anger. "'Dreary'?" The Lodge mansion was enormous, filled with expensive furniture and light. Not to mention the in-home theater, the pool, and the library full of books. "My money paid for this 'dreary' house!"

"And you know, Veronica was right," Mrs. Lodge said, ignoring her husband's anger. "It cheered me right up!" She gave him a peck on the cheek, then waved at the three trunks. "These can go to the master bedroom," she told the delivery-men. "The elevator is in the rear."

"I suppose Veronica needed to be cheered up, too?" Mr. Lodge demanded, eyeing Veronica's bags.

"Really, Daddy!" Veronica cried. "You didn't expect me to let Mummy go shopping *alone*, did you?"

"Hiram, only you could be so cruel," Mrs. Lodge said, shaking her head at her husband.

Mr. Lodge let out a groan. He couldn't win, and he knew it.

"Just wait until you see all of the wonderful bargains we got," Veronica told her father. "You'll be proud of us."

"Your daughter is a black-belt shopper," Mrs.

Lodge put in. "Veronica, darling, run upstairs and try on that gorgeous purple dress we found."

"Back in a sec!" Veronica grinned as she grabbed a pile of bags in each hand and darted upstairs. She couldn't wait to put the purple dress on again. Daddykins would probably throw a fit when he saw the price tag, and Veronica knew that she would have to sweet-talk him for hours to convince him to let her keep the dress. But it would be worth it. Because this wasn't just any old dress. This was The Dress. The dress for the Spring Formal, Riverdale High's biggest dance of the year, which was coming up the following month.

"Hello, comfortable old room!" Veronica sang as she walked into her enormous bedroom and plopped her bags onto her white embroidered bedspread. True, she had enjoyed staying at a five-star luxury hotel in Paris for a few days. But she had missed the familiar things—her fluffy down pillow, her soft slippers, her electrified closet that was almost as large as South Dakota. Veronica tucked a long strand of black hair behind her ear and kicked off her pointy black mules. "There you are!" she said to the small, silver cell phone that was perched on her nightstand, plugged into a recharger. "I thought I'd left you in an airport." Pressing the button to hear her voice mail messages, Veronica held the phone to her ear.

"You have forty-seven messages," the cell phone's mechanical voice informed her.

"That's what happens when you go two and a half days without answering the phone," Veronica said impatiently to herself.

Still, she couldn't suppress a self-satisfied smile. She was sure that at least half of the messages were from Archie Andrews. Archie was sort of her boyfriend. That is, she liked him, and he liked her . . . but Veronica didn't like for Archie to feel too comfortable. For one thing, he was girl crazy. And the minute he thought he had Veronica wrapped around his little finger, Archie started looking for other girls. That was why Veronica hadn't even told him when she and her mother took off for Paris. I'll let him wonder where I am all weekend, Veronica had thought.

Sure enough, Archie's voice was the first one on the voice mail. "Hey, Ronnie," the message said casually, "I was wondering whether you were going to the Spring Formal. Because I am. And if you were going, I thought maybe we could go together. You know, as dates."

Veronica rolled her eyes. Archie was sweet, but he wasn't exactly Mr. Smooth.

"Anyway, call me when you get a chance," Archie's voice said. "This is Archie, by the way. Okay, bye."

Veronica giggled as she erased the message. Poor Archie, she thought. He's been waiting to hear from me all weekend. And he's going to have to wait a little longer.

I think I'll wait until Monday to say yes to the formal. I don't want to seem too eager.

Just then, the phone rang in Veronica's hand. She hung up on the voice mail and clicked to answer the incoming call. "Hello?"

"Ronnie? Where are you? I've been calling for days!" It was Betty Cooper, Veronica's best friend. "Nobody knew where you were!"

Veronica laughed. "I'm fine. Mumsiekins and I went to Paris for the weekend."

"Is she okay?" asked a voice in the background on Betty's end of the line. It sounded like Nancy, one of Betty and Ronnie's oldest friends.

"She went to Paris," Betty could be heard saying to Nancy. Then, to Veronica, she said, "Well, I hope you brought us presents to make up for the fact that we were worried sick about you!" she teased.

"Of course I did!" Veronica said brightly. "Where are you?"

"I'm at Pop's, with Midge and Nancy," Betty said. "We're having milk shakes."

"And fries!" Midge called into the phone.

There was a chorus of giggles.

Veronica grinned. Just what I want, she thought, a milk shake and fries. That was the weird thing about Paris . . . those French people hardly ever ate fries. It was a real disappointment. Veronica looked at the pile of bags on her bed. I'll just yank on the purple dress for Daddykins, she thought, then go join Betty, Nancy, and Midge.

"Save me a seat," Veronica told her best friend. "I'll be right over!"

"Here I am!" Veronica sang as she burst through the door of Pop's. She was carrying two large shopping bags.

"Ronnie!" Betty squealed, waving frantically from the booth in the corner. Nancy craned her neck to see, and flashed Veronica a grin that was brilliant against her dark cocoa skin.

Midge smiled as she gingerly dunked a fry in bright red ketchup. "Thank goodness you're here," she said to Veronica. "We were starting to think you'd disappeared into the Bermuda Triangle!"

"Not quite," Veronica said with a laugh. "Scooch over, Betty. I've got presents!"

"Ronnie, I was just kidding about gifts," Betty said, blushing slightly. She slid sideways into the booth, and Veronica sat down on the cracked red vinyl. "You didn't have to do that."

"But we're glad you did!" Nancy added.

"Of course I brought you guys something," Veronica huffed. "We're friends, aren't we?" She dug around in a black shopping bag with silver lettering on it. *Mode*, it said. "This one is for you, Nancy," she said as she pulled out a hot-pink handbag.

"Oooh! I love it!" Nancy said. "It even goes with the sweater I'm wearing."

"Pretty in pink," Veronica said brightly. Then she reached into a striped shopping bag. "Sorry I didn't have time to wrap anything. This is for you, Midge."

"It's beautiful," Midge breathed as she draped the soft, moss-green cashmere shawl carefully around her shoulders. Then she smiled happily.

"Wow," Betty said as she touched the feather-light fabric. "This is the softest thing I've ever felt."

"It's warm, too," Veronica added. "For cool spring nights. And—last, but not least—for our superorganized friend . . ." Digging around in the black shopping bag again, she pulled out a green-and-blue patterned messenger bag.

Betty's blue eyes widened as she gaped at the bag.

"It has about a zillion pockets," Veronica explained, "for all of your pencils and notebooks and stuff. And it's made from recycled materials." Whatever. Veronica didn't really care about junk like that, but she knew Betty did.

"It's perfect!" Betty said, wrapping her best friend in a huge hug. "I love it!" She pulled the strap over her shoulder and held up the bag for closer inspection.

Can I pick 'em? Or can I pick 'em?

Veronica couldn't help noticing how blue her best friend's eyes looked next to the swirling blue-and-green pattern.

"So, how was Paris?" Betty asked. "Did you see any of the sights?"

"Sure," Veronica said, leaning over to steal one of Betty's fries. "We saw the Claude Darmano store, the Jannel store, the huge Buona Suava store. . . ."

"Didn't you even stop to look at the Eiffel Tower?" Midge asked.

Veronica rolled her eyes. She could never understand why people always asked about the Eiffel Tower. "You've seen one tower, you've seen 'em all," Veronica said, waving her french fry in the air.

Nancy lifted her eyebrows. "So you spent the whole weekend shopping? I wish my mom would let me do that, instead of studying."

"My mom thinks that shopping *is* studying," Veronica replied with a shrug. "It's a lot of work keeping up with the trends."

Laughing, Betty tugged at her tidy blond ponytail. "Wow, Ronnie," she said, "I think I'd like your homework a lot better than mine."

"You're good at science," Veronica said casually, "and I'm good at accessories."

"Speaking of shopping . . ." Betty toyed with her straw, plunging it in and out of her strawberry milk shake.

11

Veronica raised a dark eyebrow. "You have my attention."

Betty smiled and shifted in her seat. "I was wondering if you wouldn't mind going shopping with me next weekend," she said. "I need a dress."

"Me, too," Midge put in. "Moose just asked me to the Spring Formal, and I don't have anything to wear."

"Chuck asked me last week," Nancy admitted. "And I haven't even thought about a dress."

"Let's all go," Betty suggested.

Veronica flipped her long, black hair over her shoulder. "Well . . . it just so happens that I found the perfect little thing in Paris. But I wouldn't mind tagging along."

And that way, I can make sure that nobody gets a dress more fashionable than mine!

"Great!" Betty said brightly.

"So, Betty," Veronica said slowly, "who's your date to the Spring Formal?"

"Well . . ." Betty's cheeks turned pink. "Actually, it's Archie."

Veronica felt her body go rigid. "Archie?" she repeated. "But *I'm* going with Archie!"

"What?" Betty gasped. "No." She shook her head. "Sorry, Ronnie, but he called this morning to ask if I wanted to go."

Veronica pulled her cell phone out of her bag. "He left me a message on Friday, asking me to be his date," Veronica insisted.

Just then, the bell over the front entrance jingled, and Archie himself walked into Pop's, followed by his best friend, Jughead P. Jones.

"You!" Ronnie shouted.

"You!" Betty growled.

"You'd better run," Nancy told Archie.

Jughead turned to Archie and looked at him through sleepy eyes. "What have you done this time?"

"B—B—Betty!" Archie stammered. The color drained from his face—which made his freckles stand out against his pale skin. "R—R—Ronnie!"

Veronica slid out of the booth and marched right up to him. "I can't believe you didn't even wait for me to get back to you!" she said, poking him in the chest.

"Ow," Archie said, trying to push her sharp fingernail away. "I—I—I'm sorry, Ronnie. See, I called you on Friday, and when you didn't get back to me, I figured you were mad. . . ."

"So you called me," Betty shrieked. "I can't believe I was your second choice!" She stormed up behind Veronica. "Thanks a lot!"

"It wasn't like that!" Archie insisted.

"So how was it, then?" Veronica demanded, folding her arms across her chest.

"Yes, this should be interesting," Jughead put in, stroking his chin.

"It was—it was . . ." Archie's face turned as red as his hair.

"Forget it," Veronica snapped. "The fact is, you never think about anyone but yourself, Archie, and I'm sick of it."

"Me, too," Betty agreed. "Come on, Ronnie, let's get out of here."

With that, the two best friends turned and stalked out of the diner.

Jughead snorted, and Archie wheeled angrily to face him. "What's so funny?" Archie demanded.

Jughead rolled his eyes. "You and your women problems." He shook his head. "It's always the same old story. Don't you ever get tired of it?"

Archie narrowed his eyes. "I *am* tired of it. And I'm telling you, Jughead, this is the last straw. I'm done with girls. Finished. It's over, you hear me?"

"Right," Jughead said casually. "If you can give up girls, I'll give up hamburgers." Jughead was famous for eating hamburgers. He once ate seventeen Pop's burgers in a single hour. Then he asked for a dessert menu!

"All right, then." Archie held out his hand. "Shake on it."

Jughead stared at the hand, horrified. "What?"

"Shake," Archie commanded. "No girls for me, no burgers for you."

After hesitating a moment, Jughead finally shook hands. "I'm only doing this because I know you won't be able to go more than five minutes without talking to a girl."

Archie glared out the window, where two heads—one blond, one dark—bobbed down the street. "We'll just see about that," he said.

Chapter Two

"What's this supposed to be about?" Veronica asked as she flipped her long, black hair over one shoulder and slipped into a plush red auditorium chair beside Nancy.

"I have no idea." Nancy crossed her legs and put her new hot-pink purse delicately at her feet. "All I know is that it got me out of an algebra test."

Veronica squinted at the stage, where the principal, Mr. Weatherbee, sat next to Coach Clayton, the gym teacher. Veronica had been sitting in English class listening to her teacher drone on and on about *The Scarlet Notebook*, or some such thing, when the principal's voice had come over the public-address system, announcing an all-school assembly during fourth period. Mr. Weatherbee had sounded really excited.

Betty, who was sitting on the other side of

Nancy, leaned forward to chat with Veronica. "Maybe they're announcing a change to the lunch menu," she joked.

Veronica rolled her eyes. "Right," she said sarcastically. "I'm sure they're going to tell us that they've hired a new chef. Soon, we'll be sampling some exquisite European cuisine."

"Just in time," Betty said with a smile. Lunch was next period.

"Hi, Ronnie!"

Veronica looked up to see Archie standing in the aisle, smiling hopefully at her. Jughead and Moose were right behind him. "Mind if I sit with you guys?" Archie asked. "Betty, is that empty seat by you taken?"

Betty blew out an annoyed breath, fluttering her blond bangs. "Do you hear something, Ronnie?" she asked.

Veronica rolled her eyes. "Just the buzzing of an annoying insect in my ear."

Nancy cracked up.

"Duh, that's not an insect, Ronnie," Moose said. "That's Archie!"

Jughead put a hand on Moose's shoulder. "Moose, my friend," Jughead said, "sometimes women speak in a different language."

Moose looked confused. "Aren't they speaking English?"

"Aw, come on," Archie moaned miserably at Betty and Veronica. "You guys are giving me the silent treatment?"

"Would *you* talk to you after what you did?" Nancy demanded.

"It was an accident!" Archie insisted.

"Buzz, buzz." Veronica tried to sound as bored as humanly possible.

"I wish that insect would bug off," Betty added, folding her arms across her chest.

Moose shook his head. "They *must* be speaking English," he said. "I understand the words."

There was a shriek of feedback as Mr. Weatherbee stepped up to the podium. The audience groaned as the principal tapped the microphone. "Is this on?" he asked.

"It's on, all right," Reggie Mantle shouted from his seat in the fourth row. "It's on our nerves!"

The audience cracked up.

Ignoring Reggie, Mr. Weatherbee cleared his throat and spoke into the microphone. "All right, students, settle down, settle down. Mr. Andrews," he said to Archie, "would you and your friends please take seats?"

Archie turned bright red and looked hopefully at Betty. She narrowed her eyes at him. Then he turned to Ronnie, who gave him a little "toodle-oo" wave.

"I think there are some seats near the front, Jughead," she said helpfully.

Nancy nudged Veronica as the boys trudged toward the front. A small smile played at the corners of Veronica's lips as she watched Archie's slumped shoulders.

Let him suffer. He deserves it!

"Now, students," Mr. Weatherbee went on, once Archie, Jughead, and Moose had taken their seats, "I've called you all here to introduce you to someone very special."

Oooh, Veronica thought as she sat back in her chair, this has *boring* written all over it. Well, I guess I might as well get some work done.

She dug around in her small, black leather bag and pulled out a nail file.

School time is work time. And this manicure needs some serious help!

"Mr. Evan Smart is a student at nearby White Pine High, and he has come here today to tell us about his baseball

19

program for children," Mr. Weatherbee continued.

Baseball? Veronica thought as she sawed at her thumbnail. I'm missing *The Scarlet Notebook* for *this*? She sighed.

Mr. Weatherbee droned on for a while about Mr. Smart and his fabulous baseball program. It was supposed to benefit underprivileged kids or something, from what Veronica could gather. Of course, she wasn't listening very closely. She was too busy trying to figure out whether she should go for a French manicure or a fun color like pink when she went to the spa after school. . . .

"And without further ado, let me introduce Mr. Evan Smart!" Mr. Weatherbee said. The auditorium applauded politely—everyone except for Veronica, who was busy with her emery board.

"Thank you," said a deep, velvety voice over the speakers.

Next to her, Nancy let out a low whistle.

Veronica looked up at her friend. "What?" she whispered.

Waggling her eyebrows, Nancy nodded at the podium.

And that was when Veronica saw him.

It was almost as though the whole auditorium

went dark, except for a spotlight on Evan. He was speaking, his red lips were moving, but Veronica barely heard the words.

"Ronnie, you dropped your emery board," Nancy murmured.

Mr. Evan Smart is a hottie and a half!

Veronica flapped her hand at Nancy and shushed her. She wanted to catch every syllable that was coming out of Evan Smart's mouth.

Evan's green eyes crinkled with concern. "So you see, these kids need activities to boost their self-esteem," he said into the microphone. He flashed a winning, pearly white smile. "And I know that there are some of you out there who can help."

I can help! Veronica thought, straightening in her chair. I'd love to help! She'd never thought about it before, but now that Evan mentioned it, Veronica could see how important baseball was. Kids need baseball! she thought, staring at Evan's wavy brown hair. And they need me and Evan to teach them. . . .

Yes, that's it! Veronica imagined herself telling a group of beaming seven-year-olds. That's how you hit a touchdown! She could see the wind streaming through her dark hair as she demonstrated proper baseball techniques . . . whatever those might be.

Oooh, Ronnie, Evan would say, *you're such an inspiring example.*

Veronica imagined herself peering into those green, green orbs. Thanks, Evan, she'd say, fluttering her lashes. I know. . . .

"Ronnie? Ronnie?"

Blinking, Veronica looked up into Nancy's dark eyes.

"Are you okay?" Nancy asked.

"Of course," Veronica replied. "Why?"

The auditorium was empty except for Nancy, Betty, and Veronica.

"Because the presentation ended five minutes ago," Betty pointed out.

"Hurry up!" Betty urged as she hustled down the hall. She hitched her green-and-blue messenger bag higher up on her shoulder. "You're dragging your heels, Ronnie!"

Normally, Veronica would have been annoyed at Betty for rushing her, but she was still half lost in her daydream about Evan. "What's the rush?" she asked.

"I want to get to the baseball volunteer sign-up

table before everyone else does," Betty said as she strode down the hall toward the cafeteria.

"Hmmm . . . I was thinking baseball looked mighty good, myself," Nancy said with a knowing wink.

Betty giggled, and Veronica stopped in her tracks. "Wait a minute," she snapped.

Turning, Betty and Nancy both gave her quizzical looks.

"You're volunteering to help the baseball team?" Veronica asked Betty. "*Evan's* baseball team?"

Betty shrugged. "Of course," she said. "This totally has my name written all over it. Basketball season is over, and I've been looking for a new sport. Besides . . ." She blushed a little and grinned. ". . . It's for a good cause."

Oh, no, she isn't!

"And the coach is a total hottie," Nancy put in.

"That helps," Betty admitted, and the two dissolved in giggles.

"But—but—but what about Archie?" Veronica sputtered.

Betty's expression darkened. "Archie?" she said

slowly. "Yeah—Archie. You're right, Ronnie. This is the perfect way to show him that he isn't the only guy in town!" Betty planted her hands on her hips, and her blue eyes gleamed. "Why have I been wasting all of my energy on Archie when there are supercool, supercute guys like Evan around?"

No! No! No! You're not getting to Evan first!

"Hear, hear," Nancy agreed.

Betty started to turn back toward the cafeteria, but Veronica held up her hand. "Hold on a sec," Veronica said. "Just wait a minute." She folded her arms across her chest. "You can't volunteer to help Evan."

Betty raised an eyebrow. "Why not?"

"Because *I'm* going to," Veronica said simply.

"You're going to volunteer to help coach a baseball team?" Betty scoffed, as though this were the most ridiculous thing she had ever heard in her life.

"Do you even know how to play baseball?" Nancy sounded doubtful.

"What's to know?" Veronica demanded, tossing her hair. "Throw, hit, kick a field goal . . ."

"Field goals are football," Betty said, correcting her.

"What's the difference?" Veronica snapped. "The point is—I'm going to volunteer because I saw Evan first."

Betty glared. "You did not."

"Did, too." Veronica's dark eyes flashed dangerously.

"Whoa, whoa, whoa," Nancy said, holding up a hand. "You both saw him at the same time—remember? Just now, in the auditorium?"

But Veronica wasn't listening. She was too busy staring down her best friend. Her dark eyes locked on to Betty's blue ones for a minute . . . in the next, the two girls both sprinted down the hall.

"Get out of my way!" Veronica screeched as she barreled toward the cafeteria. "I'm signing up first!"

Betty's ponytail flew out behind her as she streaked ahead. "Forget it, Ronnie!" she shouted. "You're too slow—that's what you get for wearing high-heeled shoes to school!"

The girls rounded the corner at the same moment and skidded to a stop. Veronica had to struggle to catch her breath. There he was . . . Evan the Gorgeous was sitting at a long table. A ten-year-old boy in a baseball cap was sitting right beside him, behind a sign that read, YOUTH LEAGUE BASEBALL VOLUNTEER SIGN-UP.

Veronica was breathing hard as she and Betty strolled oh-so-casually over to the sign-up table. A bead of perspiration trickled down the back of her neck, and Veronica wrinkled her nose. That Betty, she thought furiously. She made me sweat!

"Hi, Evan!" Betty gave the baseball coach a huge smile as she walked up to the table. "My name is Betty Cooper, and I've come to sign up to help coach the team."

Evan looked up from his clipboard with those emerald eyes. "Great!" he said, flashing a megawatt grin that was brilliant against his tanned skin. "A few people have signed up to help volunteer for team fund-raisers, but we seriously need help with the team."

"Well, help has arrived," Betty joked as she leaned over to add her name to the sign-up sheet.

Grrr! Veronica thought as she watched Betty. What a kiss-up! Well, I can do better than that.

"I'm here to volunteer, too," Veronica said sweetly, batting her long lashes. "My name is Veronica Lodge," she added, putting a little extra emphasis on her last name. Most people in town knew who her father was.

But Evan's expression didn't change. "Great, Veronica, just add your name to the list."

The little boy at Evan's elbow lifted his eyebrows. Curly brown hair poked out from beneath his navy blue baseball cap, and his face was a mass of freckles. "You don't look very athletic to me," he said to Veronica.

Betty cracked up, and Veronica shot her a glare, then narrowed her eyes at the kid. "Looks can be deceiving, little boy," she said.

"I'm a girl."

"Well, then, I think you've just proven my point," Veronica said haughtily, although secretly, she was dying of embarrassment. Boy, girl, she thought defensively. How can you tell, when they're wearing a baseball cap and no lipstick?

"Don't mind Bernie," Evan said smoothly, giving the little girl a wink. "We need all the help we can get. You don't have to be an expert."

"Well, that's lucky," Betty said drily, eyeing Veronica.

"Can you even throw?" Bernie asked Veronica.

Veronica gave Bernie a heavy-lidded

I throw parties all the time.

look. "Of course I can throw," she snapped.

"I'm sure you'll be great," Evan said sweetly. A dimple showed in his cheek as he smiled.

Veronica heard Betty give a little sigh. Oh, no, you don't, Veronica thought as she leaned over and signed Evan's sheet with a flourish, adding her home phone number, cell phone number, fax number, and pager number.

Just then, Archie, Moose, and Jughead walked by. "I'm telling you, this is cruel and unusual punishment," Jughead was saying.

"I didn't make you give up hamburgers," Archie told him.

"It's one thing to give them up," Jughead said. "It's another thing to watch Moose devour a delicious mountain of them. . . ." Leaning over, Jughead sniffed the pile of hamburgers that Moose had stacked on his tray.

"Coach says I have to eat lots for spring training," Moose said. "I don't even like hamburgers that much."

"Blasphemy!" Jughead cried. "These juicy hamburgers deserve to be eaten by someone who appreciates them." In a flash, he grabbed a hamburger from Moose's tray.

"Duh—hey!" Moose cried. "Give that back!" Moose lunged toward Jughead, but stopped uncertainly after a moment. After all, he was holding a tray. Moose couldn't figure out how to make Jughead give back the hamburger without using his hands.

Just then, Archie noticed Veronica signing Evan's sheet. He stopped and stared at the sign taped to the front of Evan's table. "What's going on?" Archie asked, wide-eyed. "Ronnie, are you signing up for . . . baseball?"

"That's right," Veronica said, sticking the cap back on her pen.

"Ronnie and I are both signing up," Betty put in. "We thought it looked like Evan needed a little . . . help."

Archie's eyes flickered to Evan's chiseled face.

"Hi," Evan said with a friendly smile.

Veronica had to suppress a giggle as the color drained from Archie's face.

How does it feel to have competition, Archiekins?

"Oh, dear," Jughead said. He handed the burger to Archie, who looked down at it miserably. "It looks like you need this more than I do," Jughead explained.

"What for?" Archie asked.

"To take your mind off your girl problems," Jughead said. He sighed. "Now all I need to do is figure out how to take my mind off hamburgers."

Veronica stole a glance at Evan's face. Well, I've thought of *one* way to take my mind off my Archie problems. One very cute way!

Chapter Three

"Are you sure this is the place?" Smithers asked Veronica as he slowed the limo in front of a ragged-looking baseball diamond. Weeds choked the edges of the chain-link fence that enclosed a green field dotted with a dusty brown patchwork of dirt. Kids were running about wildly in no particular order—some were playing catch, some were diving after ground balls, some were batting. The whole thing struck Veronica as being quite dirty and messy . . . and possibly very loud. Maybe this wasn't a good idea, after all. She had on a designer workout ensemble—red with a black stripe down either side—and she didn't want to mess it up. Veronica was about to tell Smithers to pull away when she caught sight of Evan.

He was kneeling beside a chubby kid with dark hair, who held a bat in his hand. Evan was nodding, explaining something to the kid. Veronica felt her heart melt at the sweet sight.

"This is it," Veronica said. "This is the place."

With a nod, Smithers stopped the limousine, and Veronica opened the door to get out.

Crack! Thud!

Veronica threw up her hands to cover her face as she ducked to avoid a ball coming straight toward her.

"Look out!" the chubby kid hollered, but it was too late. The ball had smashed into the side of the limo.

"What happened?" Smithers shouted as he jumped out of the limo. He inspected the door where the baseball had hit as the chubby kid came rushing up.

"Sorry!" he panted, smiling up at Veronica. There were deep dimples in his cheeks, and Veronica couldn't help liking him right away. "Sorry. My name's Ernesto." He glanced nervously at the side of the limo. "I hope I didn't wreck your car."

"You should be more careful, young man," Smithers snapped.

"It's all right, Smithers," Veronica said smoothly.

"I'm sure Ernesto didn't hit the limousine on purpose."

Ernesto shook his head. "No way. It's just that I always hit the ball foul. . . . I can't seem to help it."

Nodding, Veronica reached down to pick up the ball and handed it back to Ernesto. "You hit it pretty far, though," she pointed out.

Ernesto stuck out his chest proudly.

Just then, Betty pulled up on a green bicycle. "Hey, Ronnie!" she said cheerily.

"Hello, Betty," Veronica said with a smile. Hah! Little Miss Perfect isn't looking so perfect right now, she thought, eyeing Betty's outfit. (She had on cutoff sweat shorts and a grungy pink T-shirt.)

And what is with that hideous baseball cap? Veronica thought. It looks like something she dug out of the garbage.

Veronica smoothed the front of her designer outfit and adjusted her sunglasses. Even her nail polish coordinated with her red athletic shoes.

"I'll be back in two hours, miss," Smithers said as he cast a final disapproving glance toward the baseball diamond.

Veronica waved him away and started to

Poor Betty just can't compete.

walk with Betty and Ernesto toward the dugout. Evan waved his clipboard at them in greeting.

"Great!" he said, flashing his megawatt grin. "You're here!"

We're here! Veronica thought giddily. He's happy that we're here! She smiled dreamily.

"Okay, everybody!" Evan shouted. "Over here! Team meeting!"

In a buzzing swarm of shouting, jostling bodies, fifteen kids descended on Betty and Veronica. A small, skinny kid with huge brown eyes ducked behind Evan. Looking around, Veronica noticed Bernie hovering at the edge of the group. Ernesto was standing near her.

Evan looked down at his clipboard. "Betty," he said, making a note on a lined yellow pad, "why don't you help some of the kids with their batting?" He peered at the group, then counted off five kids, ending with Ernesto. "You five, go with Betty."

"Okay, everybody, are we ready for some hits?" Betty called.

"Yeah!" her five kids cheered and high-fived one another.

Veronica glowered at her best friend. Show-off, she thought.

Evan counted off another five kids. "Okay, you five, come with me to right field. We're going to practice catching."

Evan's five kids whooped and pounded each other on the back.

"What about us?" Bernie piped up, gesturing to the four kids who didn't have an assignment.

"Veronica is going to show the rest of the kids the basics of good baserunning," Evan said, peering back down at his clipboard.

Veronica shook her head blankly. "Baserunning," she repeated. She wasn't sure exactly what Evan was talking about.

"She doesn't even know what it is!" Bernie cried.

"I do, too," Veronica snapped, planting a hand on her hip.

Folding her arms across her chest, Bernie lifted her eyebrows expectantly at Veronica and waited for her to explain.

"It's where . . . you . . . run . . ." Veronica guessed, "from . . . one base to another?" She peered at Evan for support.

"You can show the kids how to lead off," Evan suggested.

Veronica blinked. As if I have any idea what that means! she thought.

Bernie snorted.

"Or show the kids how to steal bases," Evan went on, giving Veronica an encouraging smile. "Show them how to slide."

"Slide?" Veronica's eyes were wide with horror. She was about to add, "In this outfit?" when she heard Betty shout, "Heads up!"

A ball whizzed past, skipping across the turf and rolling out into left field.

"Sorry, everybody," Betty called. She turned to a tall kid wearing a baseball jersey with red sleeves. "David, that was a great hit!"

Grrr! Veronica thought as she noticed Evan smiling at her best friend.

All right, Miss Athletic. You're not the only one who can teach kids about baseball!

Sliding can't be that hard, Veronica reasoned as she racked her brain to remember how it was done. For a short while last year, Veronica had a crush on one of the Riverdale High baseball players. She had actually gone to a game or two. Sliding, sliding . . . Veronica thought. I think it's sort of like . . . falling.

"All right, kids," Veronica said brightly. "Come with me." She flashed Evan a confident grin. "I got it. No problem."

Evan winked at her. A spark fluttered in Veronica's chest as she watched him start to walk toward right field, followed by five kids. The shy kid who had been hiding behind Evan started to follow, but Evan put a hand on his shoulder. "Felix," Evan said, "you stay with Ronnie. She'll take care of you, okay?"

Felix looked uncertainly at Veronica. Bernie snorted.

I'll deal with you later, Veronica thought, glaring at Bernie.

"Okay," Felix said finally. He smiled weakly as Evan trotted off.

Evan is so wonderful, Veronica thought. He's almost too good to be true!

Crack!

"Great job, Cindy!" Betty shouted as one of her kids hit the ball deep into center field.

Bernie looked up at Veronica. "So are you going to teach us something, or what?" she demanded.

Why do I have to have a best friend who's good at everything?

37

"Oh, right. Okay." Veronica cleared her throat and walked over to second base.

You've met ambassadors, she reminded herself. You've hosted parties for the most important people in Riverdale. You can't let a bunch of ten-year-olds make you feel dumb.

"Okay!" Veronica said brightly. "Now, once someone hits the ball, you need to run to the next base, right?"

"Not if it's a fly ball," Bernie pointed out.

The shy kid who had been hiding behind Evan looked up at Ronnie with serious dark eyes. "Unless there are two outs," he said in a quiet voice.

"That's what I meant," Veronica lied. "I was just testing you. Now . . . sliding." She bit her lip, suddenly worried that she just might make a huge fool out of herself. Veronica heaved a deep breath. You can do this, she whispered to herself.

"Way to go, Daryl!" Betty shouted as another kid knocked a ball to right field.

Evan scooped the ball into his glove and tossed it to Betty, who was standing on the pitcher's mound. "You're doing great, Betty!" Evan called.

Suddenly, Veronica's world flashed red as fury

raged through her body. In the next moment, she was running.

She ran hard—as hard as she had the day that she raced Betty to get to Evan's table. Veronica didn't think about the fact that she might sweat. She didn't worry about getting dirty, or even about chipping a nail. All she wanted to do was show Betty—and Evan—that she knew how to slide.

There was only one problem. . . .

I don't know how to slide! Veronica realized as she got halfway to third base. I have no *idea* how to slide!

But she didn't have time to wonder what to do, because just then, there was a loud crack as another one of Betty's kids hit a grounder toward left field.

"Look out!" Betty shouted.

"Whoa!" Veronica cried as the ball collided with her foot. "Ouch!" Tripping, she pitched forward and fell . . . skidding face-first into third base.

My clothes! Veronica thought as she rolled over onto her side, coughing. She was covered head to toe in dirt. Slowly, Veronica looked over at the five kids who had been watching her demonstrate baserunning. They were gaping at her, openmouthed.

"That was amazing!" Bernie cried.

"Wow," Felix whispered, gazing wide-eyed at Veronica.

Suddenly, Bernie, Felix, and the other three kids let out a whoop and darted over to slap Veronica on the back.

"I thought you were a girlie-girl," Bernie told Veronica, "but I was wrong about you!"

Just then, Betty trotted up. "Ronnie! Are you okay?"

"Of course she's okay," Bernie snapped. "Didn't you see that slide?"

Veronica hazarded a look at Evan, who was grinning. He gave her a thumbs-up.

He saw the whole thing! Veronica realized. For the first time in her life, Veronica was covered with dirt—and she didn't even care.

"Okay, team!" Evan shouted from the right-field fence a few hours later. "Let's wrap it up! Everyone to the dugout for a meeting!"

"So soon?" Bernie demanded. She looked up at Veronica. "I didn't get to practice my face-first slide."

"Next time," Veronica managed to grunt as she hobbled toward the dugout. Every single inch of my body hurts, she thought miserably as she limped stiffly. After two hours of running from base to base, Veronica ached in places where she hadn't even realized she had muscles!

How did I manage to make my eyebrow muscle ache?

"Wasn't that fun?" Betty jogged up to Veronica and clapped her on the shoulder.

Veronica winced at the pain in her shoulder. "Yeah," she lied through clenched teeth. "Super fun." She sighed as she lowered herself onto the dugout bench. Veronica couldn't help remembering how—before practice—she had congratulated herself for looking so much better than Betty. But now, after a two-hour workout, Betty looked perfectly fresh. Her blue eyes sparkled, her cheeks glowed pink as she sat down on the bench.

Veronica, on the other hand, was covered in dirt; her hair was a mess, her manicure was a disaster, and she was actually sweaty!

Ugh, she thought as she tried to brush some of the dirt from her designer workout outfit. I can't wait to go home and spend about five hours in the shower.

"Okay," Evan said as he looked around at the team. "Next practice is Wednesday at four."

Veronica's eyes widened. Wednesday? she thought miserably. You mean I have to do this again? My wardrobe can't take it! My *body* can't take it! I have to quit.

Veronica raised her hand.

"Yes, Veronica?" Evan smiled at her, his green eyes shining.

Oooh, why does he have to be so cute? Veronica thought.

Those green eyes were like the waters off the coast of Greece. . . . "Oh, um . . ." Veronica thought fast. "I was just wondering when we'll play our first game."

"Great question." Evan nodded approvingly. "We've only got three weeks to prepare for our first game, everybody, so we'll really have to work hard. Okay!" He looked down at his clipboard. "Next up—we need to raise some money for uniforms and equipment. We need about a thousand dollars. Any ideas?"

Veronica looked around at the kids' eager faces. A thousand dollars? she thought. That's all it takes?

She raised her hand.

Evan's eyebrows went up, and his

42

green eyes gleamed. "Yes, Veronica?"

"I'm sure my father would be happy to donate the money," Veronica said. "I'll just bring a check to the next practice."

A murmur of excitement rippled through the team.

Evan opened his mouth to say something, but Betty cut him off. "Ronnie!" she cried, planting her hands on her hips. "The kids want to earn their own money! Right, kids?"

Bernie looked at her blankly. "We do?"

"Of course you do!" Betty insisted. "It's good for team spirit!"

Veronica rolled her eyes. That is *so* Betty, she thought. To make things hard when they could be easy! She was about to tell her best friend to grab a clue and take the money, when Evan piped up.

"Yes—of course—" he said quickly. "Betty's right. We're going to do this ourselves. So—who's got a fund-raising idea?"

"We could have a car wash," Ernesto suggested, digging his hands deep into his pockets.

"Good idea." Nodding, Evan scribbled a note on his yellow pad. "Any other suggestions?"

"We could give people makeovers," Veronica

suggested, with a flirty smile at Evan.

"Hmmm." Evan's pen hovered over his pad, and he pressed his lips together. "Maybe we want something with more general appeal. . . ." he said gently.

"There are *lots* of people in Riverdale who need a makeover," Veronica insisted.

"What about a bake sale?" Betty suggested.

"Perfect!" Grinning, Evan tapped his clipboard with his pen. "It's easy, and we could start right away. Betty, you're brilliant!"

Veronica scowled as Betty flushed with pride. Bake sale? Veronica thought. What kind of an idea is that? It's been done a million times!

"We could even start tomorrow," Betty went on. "At the high school. I know tons of people who'd buy a snack after school."

Evan's green eyes glowed with excitement. "The middle school gets out fifteen minutes before Riverdale High," he pointed out. "What do you say, team? Could a couple of you make it over to Riverdale High tomorrow?"

"I could," Bernie volunteered.

"Me, too," Ernesto piped up.

"I could make it." This was from the kid named

Daryl, who looked down as he spoke.

Evan jotted down the names. "We need one more, I think."

"I could come." Felix blinked shyly at Veronica.

"Great!" Evan ran a hand through his wavy hair. "Now—all we need is some food to sell."

"I'll bake some cookies," Betty said quickly. "Chocolate-chip. I could make a couple dozen."

"My mom makes great brownies," Jessie put in.

A few more kids volunteered to bring treats.

"I'll bake something," Veronica said.

A smile played at the corners of Betty's mouth. "You?" she teased.

"Of course!" Veronica insisted. "Put me down for five dozen cupcakes."

Evan's eyebrows flew up as he made a note. "Wow, Ronnie," he said, clearly impressed. "That's great—thank you."

"No problem," Veronica said, giving her black hair a playful toss. She smiled smugly at Betty, who giggled.

Impressing Evan will be a piece of cake, Veronica thought. A piece of *cupcake*.

Now all I have to do is learn how to bake.

Chapter Four

"Okay," Nancy said as she sat perched on a stool at the counter in Veronica's kitchen. "What should a batter do if the catcher drops a pitch on the third strike?"

"Third strike?" Veronica repeated. "Doesn't that mean you're out?" She raised an eyebrow and looked at Nancy accusingly. "The batter should go sit down, right? Is this a trick question?"

Nancy shook her head, smiling. "Ronnie, the answer is in chapter one. Are you sure you've been reading this book?" she asked, holding up Veronica's copy of *Baseball for Ding-dongs*.

"I've been trying!" Veronica threw up her hands in frustration. "But the dumb book is so boring I keep falling asleep!"

"Okay, if the catcher drops the ball on the third strike, the batter can run to first—as long as no one is on base," Nancy said patiently. "If the catcher doesn't throw him out, the runner is safe."

Veronica rolled her eyes. "That rule makes absolutely no sense."

Shrugging, Nancy plopped the book down onto the counter. "I don't make 'em up. I just read 'em out loud."

Veronica leaned over to peer into the oven window. "I can't see a thing in there," she griped. "How am I supposed to know if my cupcakes are baking?"

With a light sigh, Nancy hopped off her stool and walked over to the stainless steel gourmet oven. "See this switch right here?" Nancy asked, pointing to a panel at the front of the oven. She flipped a black switch labeled LIGHT, and a light came on inside the oven. "*Voilà.*"

Veronica squinted at the cupcakes. "Aren't they supposed to be a little more . . . fluffy? I never should have volunteered to bake something on Gaston's day off!"

"I'm sure they'll be fine," Nancy said, flipping off the switch. "Give them a few more minutes."

Just then, Veronica caught sight of herself in the surface of the oven and gasped. "I'm a wreck!"

she cried. Chocolate batter was stuck in her hair and smeared across the front of her designer apron.

"Everyone gets messy when they bake," Nancy said.

Veronica sighed impatiently. "I just really want these cupcakes to be perfect," she said.

"I know." Nancy nodded sympathetically.

"It's bad enough that Betty is practically a baseball superstar," Veronica grumbled. "But everybody knows that her chocolate-chip cookies are the best in Riverdale." She rolled her eyes. "How am I supposed to compete with that?"

"I'm sure your cupcakes will be good, too," Nancy said loyally.

Suddenly, the timer went off. Grabbing the oven mitts, Veronica yanked open the oven door and pulled out a tray of cupcakes. She and Nancy stared at the treats for a moment.

"Well—they smell good." Nancy looked dubious.

"Do these look right to you?" Veronica asked.

Nancy cleared her throat. "Sure," she said slowly, "if you're going to use them for hockey pucks."

Veronica flipped over the tray, and the cupcakes fell onto the kitchen counter with a thud and a clatter. Picking one up, she bounced it against the floor, where it landed with a clang and cracked in half.

"This is hopeless!" Veronica shouted, pulling off her mitts and throwing them onto the floor. "I can't sell these at the bake sale!"

A smile tugged at the corners of Nancy's mouth. "You could sell them as paperweights," she suggested.

"That is not funny!" Veronica roared. She plunged her hands into her hair and gave it a yank. "Evan is going to take one bite of Betty's cookies and forget all about me! Why did I ever think that I could compete with Betty on her own turf?"

Nancy put a gentle hand on Veronica's shoulder. "Well . . . maybe you should change the game. You don't have to compete with Betty."

"I don't?" Veronica repeated. She had never thought of it that way. Not compete with Betty. Of course . . . Her dark eyes lit up. "You're right—I don't! Nancy, you're a genius!" Yanking her cell phone out of her pocket, Veronica searched through her address book.

Nancy's dark eyebrows drew together in confusion. "Who are you calling?"

"François LeGrande," Veronica replied as she found the number she was looking for and pressed SEND.

"That French guy from the Celebrity Chef Channel?" Nancy asked. "What for?"

"Because why should I try to compete with Betty's famous chocolate-chip cookies," Veronica asked, "when I can have a famous chef do it?"

"I hope you know what you're doing." Nancy leaned against the kitchen counter and fiddled with one of the rock-hard cupcakes.

"I don't," Veronica said. "But I'm sure François does. Hello, François?" she said into the phone. "Darling, how are you? It's been such a long time!" She gave Nancy a wink. "How do you like working for Daddy's TV network? Really? Good. Listen, François, I have a teensy-weensy favor to ask. . . ."

"Let's set it up right here," Betty was saying as Veronica walked toward the exit doors of the gym. The bell signaling the end of classes had rung five minutes before. Ernesto and Bernie were already helping Betty set up a long table at the side of the doors. Daryl and Felix were using vibrantly colored markers to make a large sign that read, CATCH THE BASEBALL BAKE SALE.

Leave it to Betty to come up with the perfect location for a bake sale, Veronica thought, rolling her eyes. All of the kids who took school buses used the gym exit. And all of the kids who played after-school sports would have to pass the table on their way inside. Brilliant, as usual, Veronica thought. But she couldn't help smiling.

So what if Betty has brains? She doesn't have a celebrity chef!

"Hi, Betty," Veronica said as Betty laid a paper tablecloth over the folding table.

"Ronnie!" Betty grinned, brushing her blond bangs out of her eyes. "You're just in time to help us put up the sign."

Felix smiled as he and Daryl walked over with their poster.

"What do you think?" Betty asked.

"Looks good." Veronica motioned with her hand. "Maybe a little to the left."

Felix and Daryl adjusted the sign, and Betty taped it to the table.

"Wow, those cookies look de-lish," Veronica said as Betty placed an enormous tray of chocolate-chip cookies near the front of the table.

"Thanks." Betty smiled warmly as she adjusted the tag that read: COOKIES, 50¢. "Bernie's mom made some really great-looking brownies."

"I added the frosting on top," Bernie informed Veronica, pointing to the fudgey treats.

"And I made some marshmallow treats," Daryl put in.

"Man, I'm having one of those!" Ernesto's eyes were wide. "I'm having one of everything!"

"A lot of the team parents brought over goodies," Betty said as she laid them all out on the table. She looked at Veronica's empty hands, and her eyebrows drew together. "But wait—where are the cupcakes?"

"Don't worry," Veronica said smoothly. "They'll be here."

Just then, a white limousine pulled up to the curb, and a man in a white apron and a white chef's hat stepped out. He had dark eyes and a thin mustache. He snapped his fingers, and an assistant tumbled out of the car carrying a large box.

"Oh, look." Veronica waved to the man in the apron, and he waved back. "Here come the bake-sale goodies now!"

"Whoa," Daryl whispered.

"Where should I set up?" François demanded as he walked up to Veronica.

"There's a space here at the end of the table," Veronica said, pointing it out.

François clapped, and his assistant—a slender young man with thick glasses—began pulling things out of the box. He pulled out a portable stove with two burners; two large, flat-bottomed pans; a large orange bowl with a lid, and several small plastic containers containing various ingredients. "We will need a bigger table," François announced, clapping twice.

"Bigger table!" the assistant shouted, clapping.

The chauffeur jumped out of the limousine and ran to the trunk, from which he pulled out a long folding table.

Betty gaped as the chauffeur darted over with the table and began to set it up. "What is this?" Betty demanded. "Ronnie, what happened to the cupcakes?"

"I don't do cupcakes," François announced.

"François doesn't do cupcakes," the assistant agreed, shaking his head.

"Betty, cupcakes are *over*," Veronica explained,

tossing her long hair. "They're totally last year. François won't touch them."

Bernie raised an eyebrow. "So—what are we having?"

François peered down his nose at her. "Crêpes."

"What?" Ernesto asked. He stared as François's assistant lit the burners on the stove. "What's 'crêpes'?"

"They're like a thin pancake," Veronica explained. "You fill them with stuff, then roll them up."

The kids gawked at her blankly.

"They're *French*," Veronica added, exasperated. "They're delicious!"

Jeez, don't these kids know anything about food?

"Hey, Betty!" Betty and Veronica's friend Ethel walked up to the table. "Can I buy one of these cookies?"

"Sure," Betty said. "Fifty cents."

"Don't you want to try a crêpe?" Veronica asked as Ethel handed over the money.

Ethel looked doubtful. "What flavor?"

"Mango mushroom," François said.

"It's all the rage in Paris," his assistant added.

"I think I'll stick with the cookie, thanks." Ethel

54

smiled at Betty and walked away.

Well, you can't expect a girl like Ethel to know anything about crêpes, Ronnie thought. She has zero style. I'm sure once the fashionistas of Riverdale realize that François LeGrande is here, my crêpes will go like . . . hotcakes!

"Get your chocolate brownies!" Bernie shouted as a crowd of Riverdale High students crowded around the table. "Get your marshmallow treats!"

"Get your gooey brownies smothered in rich dark chocolate!" Ernesto added. "Get your spicy gingerbread men bursting with cinnamon flavor and dusted with a light, sparkly coating of powdered sugar!"

Veronica rolled her eyes. These kids were starting to drive her a little crazy. They'd been acting as bake-sale barkers for the last hour and a half. Although she had to admit it, Ernesto had a gift for describing food. He'd tasted everything on the table, and his vivid descriptions did seem to sell treats. Maybe he could be a food critic, Veronica thought. "What about the crêpes?" she asked Ernesto.

"Get your crêpes," Ernesto called out. He didn't

sound very enthusiastic. He sounded bored.

Veronica gritted her teeth. So far, she'd only sold one crêpe. And that was to the French teacher, Mademoiselle Richard. Meanwhile, the other treats were flying off the table.

"Three cookies and a marshmallow treat," Betty said to a tall boy with dark brown hair. He was in Veronica's math class and his name was Jake. "That's two dollars."

"Thank you," Felix whispered to Jake as he took the money and placed it in the cash box.

"You've got to get a brownie," Ernesto told Jake. "They're awesome!"

"Really?" Jake asked. "Okay, add two brownies to the tab."

"That's another dollar-fifty," Betty said.

"Thanks." Felix said.

Veronica narrowed her eyes. They made it look so easy. "Jake!" she called, batting her eyelashes. "Don't you want to try a crêpe?"

Jake shifted on his feet uncomfortably. "Uh—I think I'm all set."

Grrr! Veronica tapped her foot impatiently as

Jake hurried away. There has to be some way to get rid of all these crêpes!

"Hello, Betty. Hello, Veronica." Jughead grinned smoothly and leaned against the tables. "And how are you lovely ladies doing today?"

"Juggiekins!" Veronica cried. Her face lit up. Here he was—the answer to her prayers! Of course—Jughead could eat the entire treat table! The guy had a bottomless stomach. He'd definitely buy a few crêpes.

"Hi, Jughead," Betty said. "Want to buy some goodies?"

"Hmmm . . ." Jughead studied his fingernails. "I really just came by to say hello."

"What?" Veronica stared at him. Since when did Jughead ignore goodies? That was like telling a fish not to swim!

"I'm not really interested in food anymore." Jughead shrugged. "I'm trying to develop . . . other interests."

Betty's eyebrows flew up. "Like what?"

"Oh, Archie gave me a few ideas," Jughead said vaguely.

Just then, a pretty girl with red hair walked up to the table and glanced at all the treats. "Hi," she said. "I'd like to buy two gingerbread men."

"That's a dollar," Betty said.

The girl reached for her purse, but Jughead stopped her. "Please," he said, flashing her a suave smile. "Allow me." With a deft move, he reached for his wallet and plucked out a crisp dollar bill. Then he pulled out another and handed the bills to Felix. "A small donation for the cause," Jughead said.

"Thank you." The red-haired girl's green eyes were wide with awe.

"Of course." Jughead grinned. "My name is Forsythe."

Forsythe? Veronica thought. Of course, everyone knew that Jughead had a real name . . . she'd just never heard him use it before.

"I'm Amanda," the girl said.

"Amanda—that's a beautiful name. Do you mind if I escort you to your school bus, Amanda?" Jughead held out his arm, and the girl looped hers through his, giggling.

Betty and Veronica both stared after them, speechless.

"That was weird," Veronica said finally.

"Definitely," Betty agreed. "What's gotten into

Jughead? I've never seen him like that."

Just then, Archie bounded up to the table. "Cookies!" he cried, punching his fist in the air. His eyes were huge. "I've got to have cookies!"

Veronica rolled her eyes. That was so like Archie, to flirt with Betty right in front of her to try to make her jealous. Well, if he knew what was good for him, he'd buy a crêpe, too! Veronica cleared her throat, but Archie didn't even notice.

"Which kind?" Betty asked.

"All of them," Archie said eagerly, reaching for his wallet. "I want three of every kind."

"You've got to try the brownies," Ernesto piped up. "They are the best."

Veronica cleared her throat again, louder this time.

Archie nodded. "Okay. Right. Three brownies. Pack 'em up. How much is that?"

"Nine dollars," Felix whispered.

"Archie!" Veronica wailed. "Don't you want one of my crêpes?"

Archie took a mouthful of cookie. "Maybe later, Ronnie," he said, spewing crumbs everywhere. "Right now I've got to get to Pop's. I'm meeting Chuck there for hamburgers." He finished the cookie, then walked away munching a brownie.

Even Archie didn't buy a crêpe, Veronica thought miserably. I must really be losing my touch!

Usually, she could count on him to do whatever she wanted.

"Hey! I just have a minute." Evan smiled his killer smile as he trotted up to the table. "How's it going?"

Ducking his head, Felix whispered something.

"He says we've made forty-three dollars and fifty cents," Daryl translated.

Wow, Veronica thought, that seems like a long way from a thousand. Evan didn't look thrilled, either. He glanced curiously at François, as though he had just noticed that he was there. "What's this?" Evan asked.

"Crêpes." Veronica sighed.

"Oh," Evan said. "Okay. Well, why don't you let me take the money, for safekeeping?"

Felix hesitated.

"He likes to keep it all together," Bernie explained. "And organized."

"Felix, I really should keep it," Evan insisted firmly. "I'm the coach."

Felix reluctantly handed the money over.

"Okay!" Evan said brightly. "Look, I've got to run. You guys keep selling, and I'll see you at practice tomorrow."

"Wait," Betty said, frowning. "Aren't you going to stay and help us for a little while?"

Evan shook his head and pointed to his watch. "I've got a meeting with the sports-equipment store manager," he explained. "He might be able to get us a discount. So—I'll see you all later. Keep up the good work!" With a wave, Evan trotted off.

That was it? Veronica thought as she watched Evan hurry toward the parking lot. All of this sweat—for forty-three dollars and fifty cents? And Evan hardly even glanced my way!

Veronica dug in her pocket and pulled out two quarters. "Betty, hand me one of those gingerbread cookies," she said, giving Felix the change.

François looked horrified. "Don't you want a crêpe?" he demanded.

"Oh, go stuff your crêpes," Veronica muttered, biting off the gingerbread man's head.

 **Chapter Five**

Buzzzzzz!

Veronica slapped her alarm clock, which continued to blare annoyingly. "Be quiet!" she hollered at it, giving it a solid punch. The clock fell to the floor and went silent.

Blinking blearily, Veronica looked around. "Why did I think it was a good idea to get up at six-thirty again?" she asked the dark room. Immediately, an image of Evan in his cute workout shorts flashed into her mind, followed by an image of Betty jogging perkily across the baseball field. "Oh, yeah, that's why!" With a yawn, Veronica hauled herself out of bed.

Still sore from the previous day's practice, Veronica pulled on a pair of gray spandex yoga pants and a pink tank top. Then she yanked on her hot-pink running shoes and did a few stretches.

She grimaced, feeling the pull in her tight leg muscles.

I haven't even started, and I'm already miserable, she thought. Great.

Fighting the urge to crawl back into bed, Veronica hurried down the front staircase, through the kitchen, and out the French doors. The morning air was cool, and the sky was just beginning to turn an orange gray. "Ah," Veronica said, taking a deep breath. "It isn't so bad, once you're outside, is it?"

Veronica walked for a couple of blocks, then moved into a slow jog. She was surprised to notice that the stiffness in her legs melted away as her muscles warmed up.

This is okay, Veronica thought as she jogged toward the park. Actually, it's kind of fun. No wonder Betty likes exercise.

Betty. Grrr. The mere thought of her best friend made Veronica grit her teeth. Okay, she knew that Betty couldn't help being herself. But did she have to be so good at *everything*? Even when Veronica hired a professional chef, she couldn't out-goodie little Miss Goody Two-shoes. And at practice! Betty could bat, and throw, and catch any ball that came her way. She actually seemed to think baseball was fun! And Evan ate it up. "Great job, Betty!" he'd said the day before. "Way to go, Betty!"

The only thing he said to Veronica was, "Could you pass out the batting helmets?"

Veronica picked up her pace as she ran into the park.

Wait until Evan sees what great shape I'm in, Veronica thought, smiling to herself.

Wow! I've gone five blocks already, and I'm not even tired!

"Hey, Ronnie!" Up ahead, a girl with a blond ponytail waved.

Veronica nearly stumbled. Betty? What was she doing there?

"Hi!" Betty called as she ran up to Veronica. She slowed to Veronica's pace and jogged alongside her. "Great morning for a run, right?"

"Uh—yeah," Veronica said, hiding her annoyance. It isn't fair—Betty stole my idea! What does she need to get in shape for? She's already in shape!

"I didn't know you liked to run," Betty said brightly. "We should go together sometimes."

"Well . . . I get up pretty early," Veronica

64

hedged, trying to sound believable.

"Oh, yeah," Betty agreed. "I'm up at five-thirty."

Five-thirty! Veronica was seriously starting to doubt her best friend's sanity.

"How far do you run?" Veronica asked.

Betty shrugged. "About four miles."

Four miles! Veronica had barely gone one.

"Listen," Betty said, "I was just about to head home. But I'm glad I ran into you. I've come up with a couple of new ideas for fund-raisers. What do you think of a carnival?"

"Hmmm . . ." Veronica said thought-fully, trying to hide the fact that her breath was coming in huffs. "I don't know . . ." *Huff, huff.* ". . . It seems kind of . . . ordinary." She sucked in some oxygen.

What do I think? I think Evan will love the idea! You stinker!

"Ordinary, huh?" Betty said. She bit her lip. "Maybe you're right. The senior class puts one on every fall. . . ."

"We need . . ." Veronica struggled to breathe. ". . . To do . . . something different. Something . . . new."

"That's true," Betty admitted. "The bake sale only raised eighty-seven dollars."

"Maybe . . . a fashion show?" Veronica suggested.

"A fashion show?" Betty thought for a moment. "I guess we could sell tickets."

"And . . ." Veronica wheezed, ". . . refreshments."

"Good idea!" Betty said, giving Veronica a light punch on the shoulder. "Bring it up at the next meeting!" She checked her watch. "Time for me to head back. See you at school!" She dashed off.

Once her best friend was out of sight, Veronica picked up her pace. That's *it*! she thought as her feet struck the pavement. Betty was driving her crazy!

"Oooh, Betty," she mimicked in a high-pitched voice, *"you're so athletic! You're such a good baker! You're such a good fund-raiser!* Grrr. It's sickening!"

I'm just going to have to work extra hard, Veronica decided. From now on, I'm getting up at five o'clock. I'm going to run five miles, and I'm going to listen to *Baseball for Ding-dongs* on my MP3 player. Then I'll have Nancy quiz me. I'm going to have every single rule memorized within the next three weeks! And I'm going to come to the next team meeting with a ton of ideas for fund-raisers. I'll have so many ideas Evan won't know what to do with himself! Look out, Betty! Here I come!

"There it goes!" Bernie shouted as Ernesto hit another foul ball. Veronica watched as the ball swung up and over the dugout, then fell, bouncing into the gutter. It hesitated a moment, then rolled into the drain. "Oh, man!" Bernie cried, throwing her glove down on the pitcher's mound. "Now we've lost *another* ball! If you keep hitting them foul, we're not going to have any left."

Veronica sighed. It was a week later, and she was watching Ernesto's turn at bat.

Ernesto winced. "Sorry."

"It's okay, Ernesto," Betty called. "You're making good contact with the ball. Now you just want to straighten it out."

Ernesto nodded, setting his lips in a grim line.

"Veronica," Evan said, appearing at her elbow. "Do you mind taking the kids out for some fielding practice?"

"Just a sec," Veronica said absently. Bernie was already winding up for her next pitch. "Wait a minute," Veronica shouted, trotting over to home plate. "Ernesto!"

"Yeah?" Ernesto blinked up at her.

"Try one thing, okay?" Veronica gave him an encouraging smile. "I've noticed that you usually take a long step when you swing at the ball. Try making it a little shorter. That might help you keep your balance."

"Really?" Ernesto looked doubtful.

"Just try it," Veronica suggested.

Ernesto shrugged. Veronica backed up toward the dugout as Bernie went into her windup. Ernesto bit his lip as Bernie released the pitch.

Yes! Veronica thought. It was right in the strike zone.

Taking a small step forward, Ernesto made contact with the ball.

Crack!

"Whoa!" Standing at third base, Felix stared, wide-eyed.

"All right!" Ernesto cried, as the ball sailed over the center-field fence. "That would have been a home run!" He grinned at Veronica, showing his dimples.

Veronica couldn't hold back a proud smile. Finally, memorizing *Baseball for Ding-dongs* had paid off!

"Wow, Ronnie," Betty said as she stared after the ball, which had completely disappeared. "Maybe we should make *you* the batting coach."

Veronica shrugged. "Hey—no biggie." She had to bite her lip to keep from grinning.

"Okay, I'd like to point out that we've just lost another ball," Bernie griped.

Veronica rolled her eyes. "I'll buy you a new one." She peeked over at Evan, who was smiling at her, evidently impressed. "I'll take the kids out for fielding practice now," she said casually, motioning for five kids to follow her deep into center field.

Once they were in the outfield, Veronica said, "Okay, Jessie, Felix, Daryl, John, and Keisha, let's get in a large circle." Everyone moved into the circle, and Veronica tossed a ball to Keisha. "Okay, now toss the ball to one of the people across from you. Let's try to keep the ball going."

Keisha tossed the ball to John.

Thwack! It hit the palm of John's glove, and he tossed the ball to Daryl.

With a smooth flick of the wrist, Daryl threw the ball to Felix.

The ball sailed past him. "Sorry!" Felix called. Turning, he ran to fetch the ball.

Jessie groaned and tugged at her long, brown braid. "Felix can't catch anything," she mumbled.

Frowning, Veronica watched Felix as he hurried back to the circle. He pulled his arm way back and tossed a rainbow to John.

The ball sailed over John's head. He shook his head, exasperated, and ran after the ball.

"He can't throw, either," Keisha mumbled. Her voice wasn't loud, but Felix blushed, and Veronica was sure that he'd heard her.

"Heads up!" Betty called as Ernesto knocked a ball into left field.

Okay, Veronica thought, I helped Ernesto with his batting. I can help Felix. "Felix," she said, trying to remember the list of tips in *Baseball for Ding-dongs*. "Remember to keep your eye on the ball. Take a step toward it, if you need to. And take your time when you throw. We're just practicing now, not racing."

Felix nodded, his dark eyes serious. "Okay."

The ball went around the circle again, and the next time it came to Felix, he caught it cleanly. "I did it!" he cried, looking at Veronica.

"Now, take your time with the throw," she said.

He did, and the ball sailed—only slightly wobbly—toward Keisha. It landed right in her glove.

Felix looked proud enough to burst. The look on his face sent a pang through Veronica's heart. He sure is a cute kid, she thought.

Crack!

"Heads up!" Bernie screamed. "Somebody get that!"

"I got it!" Felix shouted, lunging toward the ball. "I got it!" But he miscalculated, and the ball sailed over his head . . . then rolled toward the fence and slipped underneath.

"Oh, great!" Bernie shouted. "Another ball gone! Why don't you learn to catch, Felix?"

Tears welled up in Felix's eyes. "Sorry," he whispered.

"Don't shout, 'I got it,' when you don't!" Bernie hollered.

Felix looked like he wanted to curl up and hide.

"Why don't you watch your mouth, you little—" Suddenly, Veronica noticed that the rest of the team was staring at her. Betty's mouth was open, and Evan's face was pale. "Er—" Veronica decided to start again. "I mean . . . hey, Bernie—calm down. We're a team. We have to learn to get along. Felix is just learning."

Bernie's eyes flashed angrily. "He should learn faster."

"Not everyone is a baseball expert," Veronica told her.

Bernie turned and stomped back to the pitcher's mound.

With a deep sigh, Veronica turned back to her five fielders. Felix was staring at her with huge, worshipful eyes.

Well, I may not be the world's greatest coach, Veronica decided. But I guess I handled that one okay.

"All right, everyone," Veronica said, clapping her hands. "Let's try another drill."

"Okay, team, good practice today," Evan said as he looked down at his clipboard. The team was in the dugout, having a meeting. He looked up at Veronica and smiled. "Very good practice."

It really was good, Veronica thought, giving herself a mental pat on the back. By the end of it, Felix had caught more than half the balls that came his way, and Ernesto had looked like the next Johnny Damon. Thanks to me, Veronica thought. Plus, she'd run bases, hustled after pitches, and tossed a few balls—and she barely even felt tired.

Jogging in the morning helped, she thought. I think I'm getting the hang of this!

"All right—on to the next order of business," Evan said. "We raised almost a hundred dollars at the bake sale, so that's a great start. But we have a long way to go. Any new ideas?"

Veronica raised her hand. "I have a few," she said, pulling a typewritten list from her pocket. "What about a fashion show?"

The team let out a collective groan.

"No way!" Bernie cried.

Daryl shook his head. "Double no way."

Veronica looked sideways at Betty, who shrugged. Thanks a lot, Betty, Veronica thought. You said this was a good idea!

But Veronica wasn't about to give up. She had tons of ideas. "Okay," she said, "why don't we sell manicures and pedicures?"

"Um, I think you need a license from the city to do that," Betty said gently. She winced under Veronica's glare. "Sorry."

Pushing back a wave of annoyance, Veronica scanned her list. Hmmm, maybe having the kids give haircuts isn't a good idea, either, she decided. She skipped to the next one. "The kids could do chores around the neighborhood," Veronica said.

"Actually," Evan said apologetically, "I think there might be some kind of labor laws against that."

Veronica let out an exasperated sigh. What do these people want? she thought. "Well, it's better than a stupid carnival!" she snapped.

"Hey—a carnival!" Evan said. "Ronnie, that's brilliant!"

A murmur of excitement rippled through the team.

"Really?" Veronica asked. She looked around at the mass of excited faces.

"We could have a dunking booth," Bernie suggested.

"And sell cotton candy," Ernesto put in.

"We'll need games," Daryl said. "Like where you knock over milk bottles."

"Or bob for apples," Felix whispered.

Wow! Veronica thought as she listened to the team rattle off ideas. I guess everyone really likes the carnival idea!

Grinning, Veronica looked over at her best friend.

But Betty wasn't smiling. In fact, she looked furious.

Oops! Veronica thought. I forgot that the whole carnival thing was Betty's idea. Double gulp!

I'm a genius!

Chapter Six

"Are you sure Evan knows he was supposed to meet us here?" Veronica asked. She looked around Pop's. Evan was nowhere in sight. It was three twenty-seven, and the meeting was supposed to start at three o'clock. Veronica had been on time and had found Betty already sitting in a corner booth. Betty arrived ten minutes early, natch.

"I sent him the same e-mail that I sent you," Betty snapped, stirring her strawberry shake with her straw. "He said he'd be here."

"Fine," Veronica said, sitting back against the red vinyl booth. "Whatever. I guess he's just late."

"I guess so," Betty agreed.

Silence.

"Are you sure he knows it's today?" Veronica asked.

Betty rolled her eyes and took a sip of her shake

without bothering to respond.

Veronica checked her watch again. Well—Evan did have a habit of arriving late. I shouldn't be so worried about it, she told herself. Then again, this was the first meeting to discuss the carnival, and Veronica was excited. She couldn't wait to tell Evan about all of her plans . . . for the balloon-pop, the fortune-teller, the kissing booth. . . .

Of course, I'll be working that one myself!

Veronica shifted in her seat and took a sip of her soda. It was strange to be sitting in silence with Betty. Her best friend hadn't called in days, and it was starting to bother Veronica. After all, she hadn't stolen Betty's idea on purpose. It had been an accident! Not that she was about to let everyone know the truth—not when Evan was so enthusiastic about one of her ideas. Finally!

The bell over the door jingled, and Veronica looked up. Archie walked in—with Evan right behind him! Veronica started waving frantically at Evan.

The two boys waved back.

Archie made his way over to the booth with a huge grin. "Hi, Ronnie!" he said brightly. "Hey, Betty!"

Veronica rolled her eyes. "Hello, Archie." Then she smiled sweetly at Evan and batted her eyelashes. "Hi, Evan."

"Hi, Evan," Betty said, a dreamy look on her face.

"Hello, ladies," Evan said with a lopsided grin.

The smile faded from Archie's face as he looked from Evan to Veronica, then back again at Evan.

Veronica had to squelch a giggle. Archie's jealous! she thought happily. Good. Serves him right.

"Evan, I'd like you to meet our good friend, Archie," Veronica said. She took a delicate sip of her soda, finishing it.

"Hi, Archie," Evan said, sticking out his hand. "Great to meet you."

"Hi." Archie shook Evan's hand.

"You're lucky to have two such beautiful friends," Evan said, giving Veronica a wink.

Betty and Veronica giggled.

"Yeah." Archie didn't look as though he felt very lucky, Veronica noticed.

"And they're doing such great work with the kids on the baseball team," Evan gushed. "Ronnie just came up with a brilliant fund-raising idea. We're meeting to talk about it today."

Veronica looked away as Betty glared in her direction.

"You don't say," Archie said vaguely.

Evan tossed his jacket on the booth beside Veronica. "Excuse me for a minute, ladies," he said. "I'll be right back." He strode over to the counter and motioned to the waitress.

The minute Evan was out of earshot, Archie scoffed. "How can you stand that guy?" he demanded.

"What?" Betty asked.

"Evan is great!" Veronica insisted.

"He's so fake," Archie complained. "Everything about that guy is phony."

"Oh, please." Betty waved her hand and took another sip of her shake.

"Yeah, Archie," Veronica agreed. "Mind your own business. It's not Evan's fault that you're jealous."

"Jealous?" Archie repeated. He shook his head. "Oh, no. You've got me all wrong. I'm totally out of the girl game. I'm not jealous. In fact, I'm not even interested." Jamming his fists into his pockets, Archie strolled over to the counter and perched on a stool. "Two cheeseburgers and two sides of fries, please," he told the waitress.

Betty blew her bangs out of her eyes. "Can you believe him?"

"'Out of the girl game,'" Veronica repeated mockingly. "Who does he think he's kidding?"

Just then, a pretty girl with waist-length brown hair walked up to Archie. "Excuse me," she said in a soft, delicate voice. She pointed to the stool beside Archie. "Is anyone sitting here?"

"Watch this," Veronica murmured.

"He's a goner," Betty agreed, eyeing the pretty girl.

But Archie didn't even bat an eyelash. "Sorry," he said quickly. "I'm saving that space for my fries."

The girl stood there a moment, clearly confused.

"Did you see that?" Betty asked Veronica.

"I saw it," Veronica said, wide-eyed, "but I don't believe it."

Just then, Jughead appeared at the girl's shoulder. "Excuse me," he said suavely, "but if you're looking for a place to sit, there's room at my table."

"Oh . . ." The girl nodded. "Okay. Thanks."

"This just gets weirder and weirder," Veronica

said as she watched Jughead walk off with the girl.

"It's like Archie has become Jughead," Betty said. "And Jughead has become Archie!"

"I'm back!" Evan sang as he returned to the booth. He was carrying a soda and a banana split—with three spoons. "I thought we could all share a treat." He grinned, and his green eyes danced. "We need the energy if we're going to plan a whole carnival."

"That's so sweet!" Veronica said, plucking a cherry from the top of the banana split.

"Oooh, caramel sauce," Betty said, digging in to a corner. "My favorite."

Veronica smiled at Evan. He's so thoughtful, she thought. Who cares if he's half an hour late? Nobody's perfect.

Archie *should* be jealous, she decided, smiling to herself. Because Evan is Mr. Wonderful!

What a perfect day for a carnival, Veronica thought as she walked toward the baseball field. The sky was brilliantly blue, dotted here and there with cottony puffs of white clouds, and the spring air was warm and fresh. Veronica felt great. Sure, she'd been super busy for the past two weeks, putting together the carnival. Betty had taken over organizing the booths, while Veronica had been in charge of promotion. She'd managed to get Daddykins to run ads on his radio station, and she had plastered the high school with full-color flyers advertising the carnival. The team kids had gone door to door passing out flyers, and Veronica had even seen signs in the local drugstore, supermarket, and community center. It seemed as though everyone was buzzing about the carnival! It was the first big event of the spring.

And Betty had been amazing, Veronica had to admit. Even though the two friends hadn't been getting along very well lately, Betty had focused all of her considerable organizational skills on getting together the carnival booths. She'd persuaded the community center to donate its dunking booth, convinced the senior class to lend the kids the basic carnival booths, and managed to get each kid on the team motivated to take on the challenges of his or her booth. In the end, even the team parents had gotten involved. Everyone had worked like a dog.

Actually, Veronica thought as she waved at Felix—who was manning the

Well, almost everyone.

entrance-ticket table—there was only one person who hadn't really been that involved. Evan had passed a lot of his duties on to Betty and Veronica, explaining that he was busy having meetings with uniform-supply companies and sports-equipment stores. He managed to vanish every time Veronica called him for help. He seemed to have an excuse for everything.

I'm being unfair, Veronica told herself sternly as she walked between the rows of booths. Evan is very busy with the team, she reminded herself as she looked around.

I guess that's why he's not here yet.

"Hey, Veronica!" Daryl waved to her from his place at the balloon-pop. A couple of the kids had talked a local toy store into donating prizes in exchange for free advertising at the carnival, and Veronica smiled to see that Daryl had arranged his stuffed animals in neat rows behind a bold sign printed with the toy store's name and address.

"Your booth looks great!" Veronica told him.

Daryl smiled shyly. "Thanks. Three darts for five dollars!" He held up the darts.

Veronica laughed. "Maybe later. I've got to get to my booth!" She tossed her hair. The kissing booth, she thought, smiling. Veronica had spent all morning at the beauty salon, getting her hair and makeup done. Then she had chosen a cute pink sundress and a white sweater.

And maybe I'll even get to kiss Evan! she thought.

"Veronica!" A chubby clown wearing a rainbow-colored wig bounced up to her. "How do I look?"

"Fantastic, Ernesto," Veronica told him.

Grinning inside his bright red clown mouth, Ernesto juggled a few balls. "I can make balloon animals, too!"

"You're going to be a huge hit," Veronica said, smiling. She couldn't believe how hard all of the kids had worked to pull the carnival together. Everything was turning out better than she had expected!

Veronica made her way to the kissing booth, where she found Betty setting up a sign. KISSES, $1, it read.

"Hi, Betty," Veronica called out to her friend. "Cute dress." Betty was wearing a blue sundress that really brought out the color of her eyes.

"Thanks!" Betty stepped down from the chair she was standing on and smiled at Veronica. "I thought I needed to look my best. We want to sell lots of kisses!"

Veronica laughed uncertainly. "But this is my booth," she said.

Betty smiled. "Actually, it's mine."

Veronica planted her hands on her hips. "This booth was my idea, Betty."

"Oh, really? I thought it was mine." Betty blinked innocently. "I must have gotten confused. There's a lot of that going around, you know."

Veronica folded her arms across her chest. "Okay, I see what's going on here," she said. "But there's room for two kissers at this booth."

I didn't spend my entire morning at the beauty salon for nothing! she thought.

"Yes. Well," Betty said, leaning against the table casually, "actually, I've taken care of that."

"Hello, lovely ladies," said a smooth voice. "I'm here to help with the kissing booth."

"Jughead!" Veronica gaped at Jughead, who was wearing a velvet jacket and a cravat. His usual beanie was tilted at a jaunty angle, and he actually looked rather elegant.

"Jughead volunteered to help us," Betty said. "I thought it would be a good idea to have a guy here to draw in the girls."

Wiggling his eyebrows, Jughead pulled a small tube out of his pocket. He gave his mouth two squirts of breath spray. "Ready, willing, and able." He winked at Veronica.

Oh, jeez, Veronica thought, rolling her eyes. "All right," she snapped, turning to Betty. "So, just where do you have me working?"

At that moment, Evan jogged up to the booth. "Hi, guys!" he said, flashing his familiar smile. "Sorry I'm late—had a meeting with the other local baseball teams. Hey, Veronica," he added, turning to her. "Thanks so much for volunteering to work the dunking booth. Betty told me how much trouble she was having finding anyone for that slot."

"Dunking booth?" Veronica glared at Betty.

Betty grinned mischievously.

Veronica narrowed her eyes. Betty knows I won't refuse to do the booth in front of Evan! Oooh! This is *not* over, Betty Cooper, she thought furiously. Without another word she stormed over to the dunking booth. It was all set up. Keisha was already there, ready to take tickets. All the booth needed was someone to sit in the dunking seat.

Grrr! Veronica thought as she climbed into the dunking booth and balanced herself on the seat. I can't believe I'm doing this!

"Hey, Veronica!" called a voice. Bernie gave her a little wave as Keisha handed over three balls. "I always knew you were all wet!"

Veronica rolled her eyes. Great, she thought miserably. The first person in line is the only kid on the team who can really throw!

Squish! Squish! Squish!

Veronica's sandals oozed water with every step as she made her way to the table at the front of the carnival. After five hours, the event was finally winding down. Thank goodness, Veronica thought. I don't think I could have taken much more.

She'd been dunked thirty-two times. Bernie had gotten her twice. Reggie had gotten her three times. Even Archie had dunked her once!

Oooh, he is in *so* much trouble! Veronica thought, balling her hands into fists.

Achoo!

Sniffling, Veronica tucked her stringy black hair behind her ear. She tried to wring a little water from the edge of her pink hem, but it was useless. She'd have to send it to the cleaner.

And I don't even want to *think* about my makeup! Ugh!

"Wow." Felix stared at Veronica as she walked up to the main ticket table. Evan was sitting beside him.

"Ronnie!" Evan grinned hugely, then let out a laugh. "Gee—you look terrible!"

"Thanks a lot," Veronica said sarcastically.

"No, no—I just mean, you're a real trooper for helping with the dunking booth." Smiling, he shook his head. "You're amazing!"

Evan's praise sent a warm glow through Veronica's body. "Really?"

"Yeah." Evan's green eyes twinkled.

"I think you look nice," Felix whispered.

"Thank you, Felix." Veronica raked her fingers through her hair, trying to comb it into some kind of shape. Suddenly, she was feeling much happier. "You're a true gentleman."

Felix blushed.

"So. How did you make out?" Evan asked.

Veronica plunked a pile of bills onto the table. "Keisha counted it." She looked directly at Evan as she proudly said, "I made seventy-nine dollars."

"Good haul," Evan said, as Felix recounted the money and added it to the cash box. "We're doing pretty well. Daryl raised sixty-seven dollars at the balloon-pop, Jessie got fifty-four at the shooting alley. A bunch of the booths did really well. Plus, we raised a lot of money from selling tickets at the door, and we made a ton selling food. . . ."

"Hi, everybody!" Betty said brightly as she and Jughead walked up to the table. "I've got sixty-three dollars from the kissing booth."

"Sixty-three?" Veronica raised an eyebrow. "Well—I guess my booth did better than yours. I got seventy-nine."

Take that!

"Oh, that's just from Betty's half of the booth," Jughead put in, handing over a wad of cash. "I got one hundred twenty-eight."

What?! Veronica couldn't believe it! Jughead had outearned her . . . by kissing! She stared at the stack of bills. On the top bill was a name. *Liz*, it read, in sparkly purple letters. *Call me, 333-1234.*

Bernie and Ernesto the clown trotted up to the table. "I've got one hundred fifty-five dollars from selling soda," Bernie said.

"And I earned twenty-two from selling balloon hats," Ernesto said.

"Hi, Veronica," Bernie said with a sly smile. "Feeling like a wet blanket?"

Veronica clamped her lips together.

Felix was counting the money, his face serious.

"Come on, come on," Bernie urged him. "How did we do?"

Felix looked up at her with dark eyes. "If you distract me, I'll lose my place."

Bernie sighed. "Sorry."

It seems like a huge success. . . . Veronica thought. But we won't really know until all the money is counted. She crossed her fingers. She couldn't help being superstitious.

Finally, Felix stopped counting. He made a note on a piece of paper and looked up.

"Well?" Bernie breathed.

"The suspense is killing me!" Ernesto added.

For a moment, Felix looked completely serious. Then a huge grin spread across his face. "Nine hundred thirty-one dollars and fifty cents," Felix announced.

"We did it!" Betty shouted.

Veronica let out her breath. She hadn't realized

she'd been holding it until that moment.

We've got the money! she thought. Now we can get our equipment!

She was so excited she turned and wrapped Betty in a huge hug.

Bernie high-fived Ernesto as everyone let out a cheer.

I can't believe it! Veronica thought as she caught Evan's eye. He winked.

That dunking booth was actually worth it!

Chapter Seven

"I got it! I got it!" Out in center field, Ernesto waved Jessie away and ran up to get under the pop fly ball. "I got it!" he hollered, just as the ball dropped into his glove.

"Great job, Ernesto," Veronica called from the third-base line. The team was holding a mock game, and she was coaching the runners. Right now, Daryl was on second, and she motioned for him to move slightly farther from the base. Nodding, Daryl took a step toward her.

With a huge grin, Ernesto tossed the ball back to the pitcher's mound, where Bernie caught it easily. "Nice catch, Ernesto," she said playfully. "I'm glad our fielding is finally almost as good as our pitching."

"Don't you worry about the outfield, Bernie," Ernesto called. "Once I'm wearing my official uniform, I'll be looking so hot the batters will be blinded at the plate." He pursed his lips and tugged at his shirt.

"I heard *that*!" another player agreed.

"We won't need to catch anything, 'cause those batters will be too scared of us to swing," Ernesto added.

Bernie cracked up.

"Nothing's going to get by my new glove," Felix added confidently. "Right, Veronica?"

"Oh, right," Veronica agreed, a smile playing at the corners of her lips. She cast a sideways glance at Betty, who was the running coach at first base. Betty's blue eyes twinkled, and she grinned.

"Okay, everybody, batter up," Evan called from behind home plate. "Enough chatting. Let's play some baseball!"

Veronica's smile widened as Alice stepped up to the plate. Veronica had been smiling all day. She couldn't help it. For one thing, she was actually starting to enjoy this stupid game. Now that she understood the rules, she was really helping the team get better. And the kids were growing on her. She was even warming up to Bernie. But the real reason that she couldn't stop smiling was that the kids were in a great mood. It was fun to see them feeling proud of themselves for what they had accomplished with the carnival. And they were really excited about their new uniforms and equipment. At the start of practice, Evan had announced that he was going to drop off the money at the sports store that afternoon. They'd have their new things in a week—just in time for the first game!

Crack!

Veronica snapped out of her trance just in time to see a line drive shooting her way. Without thinking, she reached out and caught it with her bare hands.

"All right, Veronica!" Ernesto called. "Nice catch!"

"Maybe you should play outfield," Bernie suggested.

Even though her hands stung, Veronica laughed. "Reflex," she said, tossing the ball back to Bernie.

"Am I out?" Alice asked Evan.

"It only counts if a player catches the ball," Evan explained. "Base coaches don't count. Even if they can't help themselves from making a spectacular catch." He shot

Wow...I guess Baseball for Ding-dongs has actually altered my brain!

94

a look at Veronica, and she felt herself blush.

Casting another glance at her best friend, she noticed Betty's smile turn to a frown. Veronica sighed.

Why does Betty have to be so competitive all the time?

The team played a few more innings, and finally Evan called everyone into the dugout for a final meeting.

"Okay, everyone, that was a great practice," Evan said as the team gathered around. "You're looking really great. I think we're going to have a terrific first game."

The team let out a cheer.

"Who's excited?" Evan shouted.

"We are!" the team members hollered, exchanging high fives.

"You should be really proud of yourselves," Betty told everyone. "You worked really hard, and you deserve new equipment and uniforms. You earned them."

There were whoops and cheers.

"Okay. I'm heading over to the sports store." Turning toward his locker, Evan dialed the numbers on his combination lock and yanked it open. Then he pulled out the cash box.

"Can we just see the money . . ." Felix asked, blinking his huge brown eyes, ". . . one more time?"

Veronica giggled. The truth was, she wanted to see the cash, too. Usually, money was something she spent, without thinking.

But it's different when you earn it, she realized.

Evan gave him a lopsided grin. "Sure. You guys are the ones who earned it." Pulling a key out of his pocket, Evan unlocked the box.

His smile faltered. "Oh my gosh!" he whispered.

A chill swept through Veronica's body. "What is it?"

Evan looked up at her, his green eyes flat. "The money . . ." His voice sounded strangled. "It's gone."

"What?" Bernie screeched. Reaching out, she grabbed the box from Evan. Two quarters fell out, bouncing into the dust in the dugout. But the pile of bills that had been there after the carnival had disappeared.

For a moment, everyone stood perfectly still. No one dared to speak. Veronica's head felt light.

"I think I'm going to be sick," Ernesto said finally.

Next to her, Veronica heard Felix sniffle softly. A tear snaked down Keisha's face. Daryl was staring at the ground.

"How could this have happened?" Betty asked.

"It disappeared from right under our noses," Evan said. Turning, he slammed shut his locker. Veronica thought she saw his hand tremble—with rage, she guessed.

"But the money was there yesterday," Betty protested. "Then I took it home for safekeeping, and I handed it over to you this morning," she told Evan. "How could anyone have gotten into the cash box? You and I were the only ones who had the key."

Evan folded his arms across his chest. "I don't know, Betty," he said slowly. "You were the last one that anybody saw touch the money."

Betty's eyes widened, and the color drained from her face as all eyes turned to her.

Does he seriously think *Betty* took the money? Veronica wondered. No way!

"Hold on," Veronica said, stepping forward. "I don't know what happened, but I know there's no way that Betty did anything wrong." She looked over at her best friend. Bright tears trembled in

Betty's eyes, but Veronica saw her swallow hard, struggling to control herself. She nodded gratefully at Veronica.

"But what are we going to do?" Felix whispered.

"Should we . . ." Ernesto said hesitantly, ". . . throw another carnival?"

"Are you nuts?" Bernie snapped. "None of the businesses will want to sponsor us again. Besides, I'm not doing all of that work." She threw her glove on the ground and gave it a vicious kick.

"Maybe we could try some other fund-raising idea," Betty said.

The team groaned.

"We'll never make enough money in time," Bernie pointed out.

"We'll just have to use our regular stuff," Daryl said. "Wear our regular clothes to the game." He shrugged and looked at the ground.

This is wrong, Veronica thought. This isn't fair. She looked around at the mass of miserable faces.

These kids have worked hard, and they deserve their equipment, she thought. I can't let this happen. "I won't!" she said.

"What?" Evan asked.

He looked up at Veronica, and she realized that she had spoken out loud. "I won't let this happen," Veronica said slowly. "You kids reached your goal. You earned your money. You deserve your reward."

"So what?" Bernie demanded.

"So," Veronica told her. "I'll pay for the uniforms. My family will." She looked up at Betty, a question in her eyes. Please don't tell me not to do this, she begged silently. I really need to.

"I know the kids wanted to earn their own money," Veronica explained, "but they did that. You all did it. You deserve this. You've earned it." She held her best friend's gaze.

After a moment, Betty smiled.

Veronica heaved a sigh of relief.

"I don't know what to say," Evan said. "Ronnie, this is really generous."

"It's no big deal," Veronica said, blushing at the praise. Then, all at once, she was surrounded by kids.

"You've saved us!" Ernesto crowed.

"Thank you, Veronica!" Keisha cried, throwing her arms around Veronica. All of the others piled on as well, until Veronica was nearly crushed against the lockers that lined the side of the dugout. Even Betty joined in for a hug.

"You're squeezing me!" Veronica griped, but she was laughing. "Aaargh! I can't breathe! Help!"

"Okay, everybody, I think that's enough," Evan called.

"Aw, man!" Daryl complained as the team quieted down and the hugfest dispersed. "I didn't get my hug."

Veronica straightened up, feeling as though a smile were permanently cemented to her face. She wasn't sure she'd ever be able to stop grinning.

"Now go rest up," Evan shouted. "Practice tomorrow at four. See you all here."

The team members shouted good-byes as they hurried away.

Felix stayed behind for a moment. "Thanks, Veronica," he whispered.

Veronica ruffled his dark hair. "Any time."

With a small smile, Felix darted away. Veronica watched him until he disappeared behind the gate to the park.

"That was great, Ronnie," Betty said, coming up to her best friend.

Veronica shrugged. "It's the same offer I made

at the beginning," she pointed out. "We could have saved a lot of trouble if you had let me give the team the money to begin with."

"It's different now, and you know it," Betty said, punching Veronica lightly on the arm.

"Yeah," Veronica said, rolling her eyes. But that smile just wouldn't go away. If anything, it just kept getting bigger.

"Veronica, I wanted to say thanks, too," Evan said. "This means a lot to the kids. And to me."

Veronica beamed as she gazed up into his deep green eyes. The way he was looking at her even made her insides feel as though they were glowing.

"So," Betty said suddenly, "I guess we should head down to the police station."

"Police station?" Evan repeated. "Why?"

"To report the crime," Betty said, frowning. "Evan, someone stole over a thousand dollars!"

"Betty's right," Veronica agreed.

Evan bit his lip, hesitating. "I guess so. . . ." he said. "But still . . . doesn't this make the team look bad? I want this program to be around a long time, and we need the support of the community. Will anyone want to sponsor us next year if it looks like we can't keep track of our money?"

Betty's face reddened. Veronica knew that she was feeling attacked. After all, the money had been her responsibility, and it had disappeared. But Veronica thought that Evan had a good point.

"We should still report it," Betty said stubbornly. Her blue eyes flashed.

I know that look, Veronica thought. She knew how Betty could be. She could get so focused on doing the right thing that she missed the big picture. But Veronica also knew that Betty wouldn't give an inch, unless this were handled the right way.

"Look, Betty, who is this going to help?" Veronica asked reasonably. "The police will just see a bunch of poor kids, and they'll probably suspect one of the team."

"That's ridiculous," Betty snapped.

"I know that," Veronica said, "and you know that. But the police won't."

Betty's face softened. She was wavering.

"Do you really want to put the kids through that?" Veronica asked gently.

Betty sighed. "I guess not," she admitted.

"Okay," Evan said. "Okay. So I guess that's that."

Betty nodded. "I guess so." Without another word, she turned and walked quickly away.

Veronica started after her, but Evan put a hand on her shoulder. She felt her skin tingle at the touch.

"Ronnie," Evan said in his golden-honey voice. "Hold on."

Turning, she looked up into those clear green eyes.

"I was just wondering . . ." Evan's eyes trailed along the ground for a moment, then faced hers again. ". . . If maybe you'd like to get together sometime. Just the two of us."

Veronica's heart thudded in her chest. "You mean, go out on a date?" she asked breathlessly.

Evan smiled his lopsided grin. "I guess you could call it that," he admitted.

Now I know this smile is permanently etched onto my face, Veronica thought happily. "I'd love to," she said.

Chapter Eight

"Oooh! Look at those!" Veronica cooed as she gazed at the shoes in the store window.

"Cute," Betty admitted. "But I like the blue ones."

"Are you crazy?" Veronica demanded, planting a hand on her hip. "Orange is everywhere this season! It was all over the runways in Paris!"

Betty laughed. "Don't tell me they were wearing running shoes on the runways," she said, raising her eyebrows at the sneakers Veronica had been ogling.

Veronica shrugged, but a grin peeked out at the corner of her mouth. "Hey—if I need to buy a new pair of running shoes, they might as well be fashionable. Goodness knows, the old ones are looking pretty well busted." She thought about her old sneakers, which were almost completely worn down at the heels. Veronica hadn't believed it when she'd noticed it that morning, after her jog. She'd never actually *used up* a piece of clothing before. Usually, she just gave things away after she'd worn them once or twice.

"Well, are we going in?" Betty asked. "Or are we just going to stand here in the middle of the mall?"

"I want those shoes!" Veronica exclaimed. She was feeling almost giddy; it was so much fun to be shopping with her best friend. Things between her and Betty had been strained for so long that it was a major relief just to be doing something normal again. "We're going in!"

"Where are you going?" asked a voice behind them.

"Archie!" Veronica replied, turning. "What are you doing at the mall?" She knew Archie never went shopping . . . unless he had to get something for her, of course.

"Oh." Archie shrugged. "I needed a snack." He was munching a giant chocolate-chip cookie from Mrs. Forest's Treat Shack. "What are you two doing?"

"Getting new athletic shoes," Betty said, pointing to the display behind her.

"I want to look my best for our first game," Veronica said, running a hand through her lush, dark hair. "I need new shoes to go with my official uniform!"

"Which we're getting, thanks to you," Betty said, giving Veronica a nudge.

Archie's eyebrows drew together in a frown. "I think I missed something," he said. "I thought the team earned a ton of money at the carnival."

"We did," Veronica explained.

"But the money was stolen," Betty added.

"What?" Archie looked dumbfounded.

Betty shook her head. "It disappeared from the cash box," she said. "Only Evan and I had the keys."

"And we know neither of them took the money," Veronica said. "Anyway, the team really worked hard for their uniforms, so I said that Daddy would pay for them. Which he agreed to do, once I explained the situation to him."

And after I gave him the silent treatment for two hours!

Archie chewed thoughtfully. "What makes you think that Evan didn't take the money?"

Veronica let out a shrill laugh. "What?"

"He could have taken it." Archie shrugged. "I mean, Betty just said that he had the keys to the cash box."

Betty blinked in surprise. "That's true. . . ."

Veronica ignored this comment. "Why would he want to do that?" she demanded. "He's the one who wanted the team to get equipment and uniforms in the first place!"

"Exactly." Archie nodded. "He could have set the whole thing up."

"That's ridiculous." Veronica folded her arms across her chest. "Betty, tell Archie how ridiculous that is."

"I don't know. . . ." Betty bit her lip, hesitating. "I just never thought about it before. But, come to think of it, Evan did let us do all of the work for the fund-raiser. And he was the only other person who had the keys. . . ."

"I can't believe this!" Veronica exploded. "You know Evan would never take that money!"

"Just how well do you know this guy?" Archie asked. Finishing his cookie, he tossed the paper wrapper into a trash can.

"Well enough to know he's not a thief!" Veronica insisted. "Betty, back me up, here!"

Betty just shook her head. "I'm just saying that I don't know . . . for sure."

"Okay, that's it," Veronica spat. "I don't have to stand here and listen to this. You two are just jealous, that's all!"

"Jealous?" Betty asked.

Veronica put her hands on her hips. "That's right. Because Evan asked me out. Me, not you. So now you just want me to mistrust him, so you can swoop in and take him!"

"I'm sorry I brought it up," Archie muttered.

Betty's eyes filled with tears. "Ronnie, I'd never—"

"Oh, spare me." Veronica put up her hand. "Cut the innocent routine, Betty, I'm sick of it." She huffed in exasperation. "I'm outie." And with that, she turned on her heel and stormed out of the mall, leaving her confused friends behind.

Don't think about them, Veronica told herself firmly. They're wrong, and I'm right.

And, somehow, I'll find a way to prove it.

"This is a really beautiful restaurant," Veronica said to Evan as she looked around. Candles flickered atop tables set with ruby-red tablecloths and fresh flowers. Rich smells wafted from the kitchen. Everywhere, the young and fashionable of Riverdale sat chatting in low voices. "This mahimahi is delicious, Evan," Veronica said warmly, resting her chin on her hand. "I'm glad we came here."

"Don't mention it." Evan gestured to his plate. "Do you want to try some of my steak?"

Veronica speared a tiny bite. The flavors burst into her mouth as she chewed. "Wow," she said. "That's almost as good as what I'm having."

When Evan had picked Veronica up that night, she had been surprised to hear that he planned to take her to Monsoon. It was the newest restaurant in town, and one of the most expensive.

It's funny, Veronica thought as she smiled across the table at Evan, but I always assumed Evan was broke. But I guess he has a lot more money than I thought, if he can afford to bring me here.

See that, Betty? Veronica thought meanly. Why would a rich guy want to steal money? It doesn't make sense!

"So, tell me more about your trip to Paris," Evan said. He took a sip from his water glass.

"Oh, it was wonderful." Veronica tucked a strand of hair behind her ear as she talked about the runway shows and fabulous French shops. She'd never dated a boy who was interested in hearing about shopping—but Evan seemed to gobble up everything she had to say.

"It sounds like you had an amazing time," Evan said, once Veronica had finished her tale. Leaning forward, he put his warm hand over hers. "Almost as amazing as the time I'm having right now."

Veronica's heart fluttered. I wonder whether Evan will try to kiss me tonight, she thought, her stomach doing happy flips.

Just the way I like them—cute, sweet ... and rich!

The busboy appeared to clear their plates, and a tuxedoed waiter walked over and nodded his head. "Can I interest you in some dessert?" he asked.

Evan looked at Veronica. "Ronnie?"

"Oh, I couldn't," Veronica said, holding up her hands.

"Just the check," Evan told the waiter.

With a courteous nod, the waiter handed Evan a small black leather folder. Evan frowned down at the bill, then reached into his jacket for his wallet.

He held up a powder-blue object, about the size of a credit card. "Oops," Evan said, blushing slightly. "Got my MP3 player, not my wallet."

"MP3 player," Veronica repeated. "I didn't know you had one."

"Oh, I just got it," Evan said quickly. "I've been saving up for months. I even had to pay part of the bill in nickels!" He laughed . . . a little too loudly. Then he shoved the MP3 player back into his pocket and fished out his wallet. He took out a stack of bills, counted them, then laid them inside the black leather case.

But before it snapped shut, Veronica got a quick look at the stack of bills. The top one had a note written on it in sparkly purple letters. It was upside down, but Veronica thought she had read the name Liz, and the message *Call me, 333-1234*.

The name spun in Veronica's mind. *Liz. Call me.* She had seen that five-dollar bill before . . . in Jughead's stack when he handed it over at the carnival.

"Okay," Evan said, clapping his hands. "So. What do you want to do now? Go to a movie? Go dancing?"

Veronica barely heard him. That money was

from the carnival . . . which meant that Evan was the thief! Or was he? Couldn't there be some other explanation? The light is tricky in here, Veronica told herself. Maybe I didn't see what I thought I saw. I only got a glimpse. Maybe Liz gives out her number all the time.

The waiter appeared and took the leather case. Too late. She'd never know for sure.

"Ronnie?" Evan asked. "Ronnie, are you okay?"

Veronica looked up at him. Her stomach was doing flips again, but these weren't happy flips.

It isn't true, she thought. It can't be.

"I'm fine," she managed to say.

"So—do you want to go do something?" Evan asked.

Do something? How about go back in time?

I could just pretend I never saw that, Veronica told herself. Nobody has to know the truth. . . .

But he stole from the team! Oh, I just don't know what to do. . . .

"Ronnie?"

"Actually, Evan," Veronica said, "I think I'd like to go home."

Betty took a deep breath. She knew what to do, but

she was still nervous. What if she got caught?

Oh, stop it, she told herself firmly. Just do it. Quickly, she punched in the numbers and waited as the phone rang. Finally, a voice said, "Hello?"

"Hello, Evan? It's Betty."

"Oh, hi, Betty." His voice was warm and golden. A honeyed voice. "What's up?"

Betty cleared her throat. "I wanted to let you know that I think I know a way we can get some more money out of Ronnie."

There was a pause at the other end of the line. "What do you mean?" Evan's voice was cautious.

"Look, I have an idea," Betty said. "All we have to do is tell Ronnie that we've found a French designer who can get us some custom athletic shoes for two thousand dollars. She gives us the money, and we order something that costs five hundred. Then we pocket the difference."

"Why would you want to do that?" Evan asked slowly. "I thought Ronnie was your friend."

"Oh, please," Betty scoffed. "She thinks she's so great, throwing her money around like some stuck-up princess. And, if you haven't noticed, we haven't exactly been getting along lately. Besides, it's not like it'll make any difference to Ronnie. The

113

Lodges have so much money they'll never even notice." She cleared her throat. "I thought that we could split the money fifty-fifty."

"What makes you think I'd do something like this?" Evan's voice was nonchalant, but Betty thought she heard an edge of excitement in it.

"I was pretty impressed at the way you pulled that scam the other day," Betty told him. "Stealing that carnival money. At first, I was mad, I'll admit it. But then I started thinking that we might work well together."

There was a long pause. Finally, Evan broke the silence. "You aren't the goody-goody everybody thinks you are, Betty."

Betty snorted. "Tell me about it. So—is it a deal, or what?"

"Yeah," Evan said. "It's a deal. But I'm not sharing that carnival money. That's already spent."

"I wouldn't ask you to," Betty said.

"It's good that the scam is a little different this time," Evan went on. "I like that."

"Yeah," Betty agreed. "This way Ronnie won't get suspicious."

"Right," Evan said sarcastically. "Although she isn't exactly a genius. I was more worried about the kids figuring things out."

"Good point," Betty admitted.

"Okay, so you find out about some cheap places we can get sneakers," Evan went on. "I'll start talking the idea up to Ronnie. That girl is practically eating out of the palm of my hand, anyway."

"Sounds great," Betty said. She held on to the phone for a moment as Evan clicked off. She took a deep breath. "You still there?" she asked.

"I sure am," Veronica said. She had been listening to the entire conversation on a three-way calling line. She looked down at the mini tape recorder in her hand and pressed the STOP button.

"Ronnie—" Betty said carefully. "I'm sorry. . . ."

"Why?" Veronica demanded.

"Well—because Evan was so—"

"Yeah, well." Veronica blinked hard, grateful that she was on the phone, so Betty couldn't see the tears in her eyes. Evan never liked me, she realized. He was just using me.

Suddenly, Veronica's sadness turned to anger. She couldn't believe this was happening. "Let's see if Evan thinks I'm a genius when he finds out that I got his whole confession on tape."

115

"Well, I think he might be singing a different tune," Betty said with a giggle.

"I'll say," Veronica agreed. "Something like 'Jailhouse Rock.'"

Chapter Nine

"Look at the size of them," Bernie said as she stared out at the other team's dugout.

Veronica followed Bernie's gaze to the place where the other team—the Cougars—were stretching to warm up. Their coach nodded at Veronica. He had silver hair cut in a military style and wore a whistle around his thick neck. Veronica thought that he looked about as scary as his team did. Betty and Veronica exchanged nervous glances. After all, it was the first game, and they were in charge.

"Are they really in fifth grade?" Ernesto asked. He pointed to a tall guy in a crisp, yellow-and-black uniform. "That guy is taller than my dad."

"We're dead," Felix whispered.

"We're not dead," Veronica insisted. She looked at Bernie and winked. "We've got excellent pitching, killer batting, and

The kid has a point.

117

serious skills with the glove."

"Not to mention speed between the bases," Betty added. "And a major cheering section." She looked up into the bleachers, where Archie, Jughead, Reggie, Nancy, Chuck, Moose, and Midge were sitting.

Veronica waved, and her friends let out a cheer. Jughead waved a homemade "Go, Eagles" banner, which made Veronica laugh. It had taken them a while to come up with a name for their team. Veronica thought Eagles was perfect.

"That's true," Daryl admitted, kicking the dirt with his beat-up sneakers.

"Where's Evan?" Bernie demanded. "Why isn't *he* here?"

Betty bit her lip and looked at Veronica.

"He really wanted to be here," Veronica hedged. "But he had an important appointment that he couldn't miss. Kind of an emergency." An appointment at the police station, Veronica added mentally. Explaining how the team's carnival money turned into an MP3 player and dinner at Monsoon.

Bernie narrowed her eyes and looked out at the other team. "If he believed in us, he'd be here," she said, an edge of anger in her voice.

"That isn't true," Betty put in quickly.

"Look, I've got something for you guys," Veronica said, pulling a box out from beneath the bleachers. She opened the lid and took out a red shirt that said RIVERDALE EAGLES, in white lettering across the chest. Handing it to Bernie, Veronica said, "This one is for you."

"It even has my last name on the back!" Bernie cried, flipping the shirt around so everyone could see. MAXWELL, it read, with the number seventeen in large type beneath it.

Suddenly, Veronica was mobbed by players, everyone reaching into the box and grabbing shirts, with shouts of, "This one's for Jessie! Pass it back to Jessie!" "Where's mine?" "Here's Keisha's! Toss it over." It was a moment of mass confusion; then Betty pulled out a box of uniform pants, and the chaos increased as everyone scrambled to find his or her size.

"Man!" Ernesto cried, holding up his uniform. "These are tight!"

"Then get a bigger size," Betty suggested.

Ernesto rolled his eyes.

"He means, the pants are 'cool,'" Daryl

translated for Betty. Then he grinned. "*Very* cool!"

"Okay, everyone!" Veronica called. "You can get dressed in the pool changing area in the club-house. It's unlocked."

"You've got ten minutes; then I want to see you back here," Betty announced.

"We've got to warm up if we want to win this game!" Veronica shouted.

With whoops and hollers, the team raced toward the clubhouse.

Betty and Veronica looked at each other and cracked up.

"I don't think I've ever seen them so excited," Betty said.

Veronica grabbed Betty's hands and squeezed them. "Did you see Bernie? She was actually smiling!"

"And Felix was strutting around like a rooster!" Betty grinned. "You did a very good deed today, Veronica Lodge."

A warm feeling swept over Veronica. I did, didn't I? she thought, smiling at her best friend.

"Even if Evan nearly ruined it," Betty added.

"I'll never forget the look on his face when we showed up at his front door with two policemen!"

Veronica said. "It was absolutely priceless."

"Yeah." Betty nodded. "I thought he was going to faint when you played the tape for him, then handed it over to Officer Stanton."

"I wonder what kind of story Evan is telling them down at the police station," Veronica said.

"It doesn't matter," Betty said, "because the tape is all the proof the judge will need."

"That's true."

It was funny. Even though Evan had turned out to be a major disappointment, Veronica wasn't very upset about it. It was true that she had only joined the baseball team because of him. But the fact was, over the weeks of hard work and practice, Veronica had come to love the kids on the team more than she ever liked Evan. She had even come to love baseball.

And there was one other thing. . . .

"Betty," Veronica said slowly, "I'm really glad you're here. And I'm sorry that I ever let a boy come between us." She looked into her best friend's eyes. "Can you forgive me?"

Betty stared back for a moment, then started giggling. The giggle became a laugh, and Betty hugged Veronica. "Oh, Ronnie," she said, her blue eyes twinkling. "It's not like it's the first time!" She glanced up into the bleachers, where Archie sat, eating a hot dog.

Veronica remembered all of the times that she and Betty had argued over Archie. It was strange, but Veronica almost missed that arguing. "That's true," Veronica admitted. She realized all of a sudden just how much she missed Archie—and all of her friends. She'd been paying so much attention to Evan lately that she'd barely seen her friends.

"And it probably won't be the last," Betty said.

Veronica rolled her eyes. "That's true, too."

"But that's the great thing about us," Betty said. "We'll always be best friends, no matter what."

"Friends till the end," Veronica added, pulling Betty close for another hug. "Friends forever."

"Come on, Bernie," Veronica muttered under her breath. "You can do it."

The muscles along Bernie's jaw rippled as she focused on the batter at home plate. It was the third inning, and Bernie had pitched well for the first two. But suddenly, at the start of the inning, Bernie had let go a wild pitch. It had hit the batter, who walked automatically to first. Then she walked another batter. She struck out one and got one out on a pop fly. But there were still two batters on base.

"Don't be nervous," Veronica whispered, trying to beam good thoughts into Bernie's brain from her place in the dugout. She cast a sideways glance at Betty, who had her fingers laced through the holes in the chain-link dugout fence. She leaned forward, watching anxiously as Bernie went into her windup.

Crack!

"I got it!" Ernesto shouted as he ran toward the center-field fence. "I got it!"

But the ball was too high. It rocketed over Ernesto's head, bounced once, and flew beyond the fence. The Cougars bleachers erupted into cheers—a triple! The two runners on base came home to score, and now the Eagles were down by two.

"Time-out!" Veronica called, trotting onto the field toward Bernie. As Veronica approached, she saw that Bernie's face was red beneath her freckles, and that she looked as though she were fighting tears. "Are you okay?" Veronica asked gently.

Bernie's mouth remained clamped shut, and

she shook her head. She looked miserable.

"You can do it, Bernie," Veronica told her. "Just one more out."

"I can't do it." Bernie's voice wavered as she glanced over her shoulder to the spot where the tall Cougar shortstop stood swinging his bat. The umpire nodded impatiently, and Bernie turned back to Veronica. "They're too good."

"Listen to me," Veronica said, looking into Bernie's brown eyes. "It's true. They're good. But so are you. We're only down by two. Do your stuff. Get this guy out, and our batters can catch up."

Bernie shook her head. "I don't know—"

Veronica held up a hand. "*I* know," she said. "I know you can do it. Everyone on the team knows you can do it. So, do it."

Bernie thought for a moment. "Sometimes you're kind of tough," she said finally.

"Only when I need to be." Grinning, Veronica stepped toward the dugout.

"Hey, Veronica?" Bernie called.

Veronica turned.

"Even if Evan isn't here," Bernie said, "I'm really glad you are."

"Enough talking!" the umpire shouted from

behind home plate. "Batter up!"

Smiling from ear to ear, Veronica trotted back to the dugout.

"Is she okay?" Betty asked once Veronica took her seat on the bench.

"Better than that," Veronica replied. Okay, Bernie, she thought. Do your stuff.

Bernie went into her windup. Like a whipcrack, she let the ball go.

"Strike one!" the umpire shouted.

Behind her, Veronica heard her friends cheering wildly from the stands.

Another pitch, and it was strike two. Veronica watched Bernie's face. Her concentration was intense as she let go another pitch.

"Strike three!" the umpire called. "You're out!"

"She did it!" Betty shouted.

Veronica nodded. The inning was over.

Now all we have to do is catch up, she thought as she headed out to her position by third base. She grinned at Bernie as she passed her, but Bernie didn't even notice. She was already thinking about the next inning; Veronica could tell.

The first batter up was Daryl, who hit a pop fly to the left infield. Out.

Felix stepped up to home plate. His large eyes seemed worried as he stared at the muscular Cougars pitcher.

"You can do it, Felix!" Veronica called.

The first pitch zipped by him.

"Strike one!" the umpire called.

Felix blinked in surprise.

Gosh, I could hardly even see that pitch! Veronica thought.

The pitcher went into his windup. Zip! Felix watched the ball go by.

"Strike two!"

Veronica felt a knot in her stomach. Ohpleaseohpleaseohplease, she begged silently.

The pitcher stared hard at Felix. And then, in a flash, he unleashed the ball. Felix swung.

Crack! The ball soared into the outfield and bounced on the grass between the center and right fielders.

"Fair ball!" the umpire shouted as Felix darted to first.

The bleachers exploded with cheers, and Veronica found herself clapping wildly and whistling. Betty patted Felix on the back.

He hit it! Veronica thought, feeling a surge of

pride well up inside her. He actually hit it!

Keisha kicked the dirt off her cleats and stepped up to the plate. The first pitch rocketed toward her, and she swung.

Crack!

The ball went deep into left field. But the fielder raced after it. For a moment, it looked as if the ball would be just out of reach, but the fielder dived for it, and it landed cleanly in his glove.

"Go, Felix!" Betty shouted. "Run!"

Veronica turned just in time to see Felix tag up and dash to second base. He made it just before the fielder could tag him.

"Safe!"

Felix beamed as the team cheered. He hopped up and down on the base a little, then grinned at Veronica. She gave him a thumbs-up.

Okay, so we have two outs and a runner on second, Veronica thought. A home run would tie up the game. . . .

Ernesto stepped up to the plate.

The pitcher went into his windup. Zip. Ernesto didn't move.

"Ball," the umpire called.

The pitcher spat and shook his head.

Now who's nervous? Veronica aimed her thought at the pitcher. We're coming back!

She knew that Ernesto could knock the ball out of the park. He'd done it plenty of times in practice. . . .

The pitcher nodded at the catcher. He was about to go into his windup when out of the corner of her eye Veronica caught a flash of movement. Felix was running toward third!

"No, Felix!" Veronica shouted. She hadn't given the signal, but Felix was trying to steal third base.

In one fluid motion, the Cougars pitcher flicked the ball to the third baseman, who bore down on Felix. Felix tried to stop in his tracks and go back to second, but his momentum was too great. He tripped over his feet and fell flat on his face.

"You're out!" the umpire shouted as the third baseman tagged Felix.

For a moment, Felix didn't even move. He just lay there, facedown in the dirt.

Veronica raced over to him. "Felix!" she shouted. "Felix, are you all right?"

Turning over, Felix looked up at Veronica. His face was streaked with tears. "I blew it," he whispered. "I lost the game for us."

"No, Felix." Veronica shook her head. "There were two outs before yours. Besides, this is only the fourth inning." She smiled at him. "We're still going to win it."

Felix blinked at her. "We are?"

Veronica grinned. "Definitely," she said.

"Just a little hit," Bernie muttered under her breath. "Just a little one, please, Daryl." She was standing in the dugout, but Veronica could hear her from her place beside third base.

It was the bottom of the ninth inning, and Veronica was starting to get tense. True, some things had gone well. Bernie had pulled it together and pitched six shutout innings. But the Eagles hadn't been able to make anything happen, battingwise. The score was still 2–0 . . . and they were running out of time.

Two outs, Veronica thought miserably. We already have two outs. If Daryl strikes out . . . it's game over. She sighed, wondering what she would say to the team if that happened. Veronica didn't like losing.

The pitcher stared at Daryl. He wound up and released the ball. Daryl didn't move.

"Ball four," the umpire announced.

"Good eye, Daryl!" Veronica shouted as Daryl flashed her a brilliant grin on his way to first.

"Okay, that's good," Bernie said nervously. "A walk is as good as a hit."

With a heavy sigh, Felix stepped up to the plate. Bernie let out a soft groan.

"Hey," Veronica said, giving Bernie a gentle nudge. "Have a little faith."

Bernie nodded. "You're right, you're right." She wiped her palms on her gray pants. "You can do it, Felix!" she shouted.

Blinking, Felix stepped up to the plate. Veronica bit her lip. Felix had struck out twice since his hit in the fourth inning. He kept trying to swing at the ball, but it was always too fast for him.

The pitcher went into his windup. . . .

Suddenly, Felix swung out sideways, holding the fat part of his bat.

Betty gasped. "He's bunting!"

"I can't watch!" Bernie clapped her hands over her eyes.

Sure enough, the ball dribbled off the bat as Daryl took off for second. Felix dropped his bat and raced toward first. The pitcher ran toward home as the catcher reached for the ball, but they got in each other's way, and the catcher made the toss to first too late. Daryl took off toward third, and made it with time to spare.

"Safe!"

"Hey, Veronica," Daryl said with a smile.

"Nice seeing you here," Veronica told him.

There was a sound like an earthquake coming from the Eagles bleachers, and Veronica turned to see Moose stamping his feet.

"Go, Eagles!" Archie shouted as Nancy let out an earsplitting whistle.

"We're gonna come back!" Betty said to Veronica. "We're going to do it—I just know it!"

"I hope so," Veronica said as Ernesto stepped up to the plate. Her heart thumped wildly. For a moment, she thought it might burst through her chest.

The pitcher's nostrils flared angrily as he unleashed his pitch. A ball. The second pitch was a ball, too.

"Way to watch 'em, Ernesto!" Bernie shouted.

But the third pitch was a strike.

"Stay cool," Veronica called, but she wasn't

sure whether she was talking to Ernesto or herself.

There was no sign of Ernesto's trademark smile as he went into his stance. He was focused.

Felix took a slightly larger lead off first.

"Don't run, Felix," Veronica murmured. "Please don't run." If Felix tried to steal second, he wouldn't make it, Veronica was sure. This pitcher was too good. It was as if he had eyes in the back of his head. Whatever you do, Felix, Veronica thought, don't strike out!

Felix scooted another inch toward second.

The Cougars pitcher went into his windup . . . then, suddenly, he jerked sideways.

A pick-off move! Veronica thought frantically. He's throwing to first!

That was clearly what Felix thought, too, because he dived for the bag. Ernesto eased away from the batter's box.

But the ball didn't go to first. It sailed over home plate.

"Strike three!" the umpire shouted. "You're out! Game over."

The Cougars cheered.

"We lost," Daryl said. He sounded as though he couldn't believe it.

Veronica *didn't* believe it. This was wrong—dead wrong!

"Hold it!" Veronica stormed over to the umpire. "That's not fair," she insisted. "The pitcher tricked Ernesto. He stepped to the side, like he was going into a pick-off move."

Betty ran over to home plate.

The umpire shrugged. "Too bad," he said.

"What do you mean, 'too bad'?" Veronica shouted. "He tricked him!"

"Ronnie, stay calm," Betty said.

"Look, lady," the umpire said to Veronica. "The rulebook doesn't say that the pitcher can't take a step to the side while delivering a pitch."

"Wanna bet?" Veronica demanded. "Try checking page 237." She folded her arms across her chest. "'The pitcher can step forward to deliver a pitch,'" she recited, "'or backward and then forward, *but not sideways*.'"

"She's right!" Nancy shouted from the bleachers. "I quizzed her on that!"

The umpire frowned. "Actually . . ." he said slowly, ". . . I think you are *right*."

That's right, I'm right!

"So . . ." Ernesto looked confused. "Do I get another pitch?"

"Batter up!" The umpire adjusted his mask.

"Are you serious?" the Cougars pitcher griped from the mound. "This is stupid! We won!"

The umpire scowled at him. "Batter. Up."

Thank you again, *Baseball for Ding-dongs*, Veronica thought as she headed back toward the third-base line.

A grin broke out over Ernesto's face as the Eagles whooped and cheered. He took the plate, and held up his bat, ready.

The pitcher glared and went into his windup.

Ernesto stared him down.

Veronica felt almost as though she were watching in slow motion as the ball sailed out of the pitcher's hand and screamed toward the mound. With a quick, powerful move, Ernesto twisted his body and swung.

Crack!

The moment she heard the bat hit the ball, Veronica knew it was a good hit. A double maybe, or a triple.

Daryl poured on the speed, crossing home in a flash as Ernesto dashed for first.

"Keep going, Felix!" Veronica coached. "Run!"

Rounding third, Felix raced toward home

plate. Score! The game was tied!

But the ball kept going . . . and going. . . .

Ernesto crossed second. . . .

The ball was still going . . . it was heading for the fence. . . .

Gone!

It was a home run! Squealing, Veronica jumped up and down, clapping, as she watched the ball sail over the fence. "We won!" she shouted. "We won!"

Behind her, the team poured out of the dugout to hug Daryl, then Felix, and—finally—Ernesto as they crossed home plate.

Veronica felt an arm drape itself around her shoulders.

"We did it," Betty said. "We won!"

Veronica grinned at her best friend. "We sure did."

 # Chapter Ten

"**W**ow!" Veronica said as she walked up to the gym doors. "You look amazing!" After weeks of wondering whether she would have a date to the Spring Formal, she'd finally found someone to go with.

"Thanks!" Betty smiled warmly as she twirled. She was wearing a hot-pink strapless dress that fell just below the knee, and her blond hair was done in an elegant updo. "You look gorgeous," she told Veronica. "I love your dress!"

Veronica thrust out a hip and tossed her hair. "This old rag?" she said drily, gesturing at the drop-dead gorgeous purple column gown she had picked up in Paris. She winked at Betty, and the two girls cracked up. "Well what do you say. Shall we?" Veronica held out her arm.

"We shall." Betty laced her arm through

Veronica's, and the two best friends strutted into the gymnasium.

"Hey, there's Reggie!" Betty said, waving. "And Nancy!" Most of their friends were already on the dance floor.

"Midge looks great," Veronica said, smiling as her friends danced. "But where's Archie?"

Betty pointed. "Over by the snack table," she said. Betty looked around, then squinted at a group of people standing in the corner. "Isn't that Moose? What's he doing?"

"Is it me . . ." Veronica asked, ". . . or does it look like he's trying to protect Jughead?"

Betty's eyebrows disappeared beneath her bangs. "I think we'd better go check it out."

Betty and Veronica hurried over to the corner, where three girls were yelling at Jughead. Veronica had to bite back a giggle when she saw him. She'd never seen Juggie in a tuxedo before. But he was still wearing his beanie, natch.

He may look suave, Veronica thought, but he seems to be having a very unsuave moment. . . .

"I thought *I* was your date!" shouted a redhead in a black dress. She was holding two glasses of punch, and it looked as though she had just brought one for Jughead, and arrived to find him with two other girls.

"You *are* my date," Jughead said smoothly.

"Wait a minute," said a girl with short blond hair. *"I'm* your date. You asked me out at the carnival!" She took a step toward Jughead, and Moose elbowed his friend out of the way.

Jughead scratched his head. "Of course you're my date; Liz, I—"

"Are you saying that we're all your dates?" Frowning, a girl with cocoa skin wearing a funky green dress glared at Jughead.

"Yes, that's it exactly!" Jughead said happily. "How could I choose among three such beautiful ladies?" He grinned in a debonair way.

The three girls looked at each other.

Wow, Veronica thought. Is that line actually going to work? She and Betty exchanged glances.

"You are such a jerk!" Liz shouted, chucking her corsage at Jughead.

"Uh, you shouldn't throw things," Moose said. "Somebody could get hurt."

"Oh, they could get hurt?" said the redhead. In a flash, she tossed both of her cups of punch in Jughead's face. "I guess they could get dirty, too."

She turned to the other girls. "Come on, let's get out of here."

"I'm right behind you," muttered the girl in the funky green dress.

The three girls stalked off as Jughead wiped the punch from his face.

"Duh, you're all wet," Moose told him.

Jughead sighed. "For once, my friend, you have a good point."

Veronica couldn't help giggling at the sight of her friend wiping sticky punch off his hair. "Oh, Juggie," she said, walking over. "Have a tissue." She pulled one from her purse.

"Thanks." Jughead dabbed at his forehead. Suddenly, his face brightened. "Say, Veronica," he said slowly. "Are you here with a date?"

"Juggie," Veronica said with a laugh, "I think you'd better quit while you're ahead."

"He's not a head," Moose pointed out. "He's a whole person. Hi, Betty. You look nice."

"Thanks, Moose." Betty smiled. "Hey—does anyone want to get some punch?"

"I've already had some, thanks," Jughead said drily.

Veronica laughed. "I'm thirsty," she said. "Let's

see what they've got at the snack table."

Moose headed out to the dance floor to dance with Midge as Betty, Veronica, and Jughead went to investigate the snacks. Archie was standing beside a nearly empty bowl of corn chips. He was watching the dancers and munching away. When he saw Betty and Veronica, his eyes widened, and he dropped the chip he'd been holding.

"Whoa," Archie said.

Betty and Veronica looked at each other, then dissolved in giggles. This was the Archie they knew!

Veronica batted her eyelashes. "Hello, Archie. Would you like to dance?"

"With both of us?" Betty put in.

"That is . . ." Veronica added playfully, ". . . if you haven't given up on girls yet."

Archie thought for a moment. "You know," he said, brushing his hands on his trousers. "These chips are awfully good. . . ." A grin broke out over his face. "But you two are way better."

Betty and Veronica cracked up, and in a moment, the three friends were locked in a group hug.

"So what are we waiting for?" Archie said. "Let's dance!"

"Juggie, do you want to join us?" Veronica asked. She looked around. Where had he gone? she wondered. "Juggie? Juggie!"

"Ugh." A groan rose from the floor, and Betty, Veronica, and Archie looked down to see Jughead lying there, rubbing his belly. "I can't believe I ate the whole thing. . . ." he said.

"Oh my gosh!" Betty said suddenly. "Juggie ate everything on the snack table! There's nothing left!"

Veronica laughed. "Well," she said, "I guess everything is back to normal. Thank goodness!"